this one's a bit
Steamy... ~~eeek~~

KISSING MY CO-WORKER ✨

by

J. Sterling

KISSING MY CO-WORKER

Edited by:

Jovana Shirley

Unforeseen Editing

www.unforeseenediting.com

Cover Design by:

Michelle Preast

www.Michelle-Preast.com

www.facebook.com/IndieBookCovers

Print Edition, License Notes

No part of this book combination may be reproduced or transmitted in any form or by any means, electronic or mechanical, including photo-copying, recording, or by any information storage and retrieval system without the written permission of the author, except for the use of brief quotations in a book review.

Both stories are a work of fiction. Names, characters, businesses, places, events, and incidents are either the products of the author's imagination or used in a fictitious manner. Any resemblance to actual persons, living or dead, or actual events is purely coincidental.

ISBN-13: 978-1-945042-43-0

Please visit the author's website
www.j-sterling.com
to find out where additional versions may be purchased.

Other Books by J. Sterling

Bitter Rivals – an enemies to lovers romance

Dear Heart, I Hate You

10 Years Later – A Second Chance Romance

In Dreams – a new adult college romance

Chance Encounters – a coming of age story

THE GAME SERIES

The Perfect Game – Book One

The Game Changer – Book Two

The Sweetest Game – Book Three

The Other Game (Dean Carter) – Book Four

THE PLAYBOY SERIAL

Avoiding the Playboy – Episode #1

Resisting the Playboy – Episode #2

Wanting the Playboy – Episode #3

THE CELEBRITY SERIES

Seeing Stars – Madison & Walker

Breaking Stars – Paige & Tatum

Losing Stars – Quinn & Ryson

THE FISHER BROTHERS SERIES

No Bad Days – a New Adult, Second Chance Romance

Guy Hater – an Emotional Love Story

Adios Pantalones – a Single Mom Romance

Happy Ending

THE BOYS OF BASEBALL

(THE NEXT GENERATION OF FULLTON STATE BASEBALL

PLAYERS):

The Ninth Inning – Cole Anders

Behind the Plate – Chance Carter

Safe at First – Mac Davies

FUN FOR THE HOLIDAYS

(A COLLECTION OF STAND-ALONE NOVELS WITH HOLIDAY

BASED THEMES)

Kissing my Co-worker

Dumped for Valentine's

My Week with the Prince

Spring's Second Chance

Summer Lovin'

Falling for the Boss

SORRY, AM I DROOLING?

✪ LILY

WASN'T THE type of woman who'd ever wanted to sleep with a *coworker*. Every job I'd had before this one, I'd been able to contain my emotions and my desires, easily separating business from pleasure and without any real challenge. There wasn't a single guy that I'd thought about outside of the office. Ever. At least, that had always been the case before I started working with Declan *I'm so ridiculously sexy that I make your panties melt with just one look in your direction* Maguire.

Now, it was all I could think about. During work. After work. And on weekends.

Screwing him on his oversize mahogany desk as folders and papers crashed to the floor around us like confetti during the Macy's Day Parade.

Him taking me from behind in the conference room as I

gripped the edge of the table for leverage, pushing back into him, the sounds reverberating throughout the otherwise empty space.

Fucking him in the corporate kitchen, where we'd first met, my legs wrapped around his hips as he pounded into me with reckless abandon.

Declan had turned me into a walking hormone factory, and I had never, ever in my twenty-eight years on this earth fantasized about a man the way I dreamed about all the things that I could do to him.

It was a problem.

Mostly because I knew it was written all over my face whenever he looked at me. I had no idea how to hide it—this overwhelming desire to drop to my knees and please the ever-loving fuck out of him. Literally. I had to stop myself from doing it each time he walked by.

What the hell is wrong with me?

And even though there weren't hard and fast rules about dating coworkers at Rockline Studios, it definitely seemed frowned upon. Especially when it dealt with a subordinate and a superior within the same department. I'd heard rumblings about some things that had happened before I started working here, but at this point, I had no idea what was reality and what was overblown fiction. We were required to attend multiple human resource classes upon getting hired and take yearly refresher courses online. I'd signed a document that stated I would let them know if someone in a position above me ever made me feel uncomfortable or made unwanted sexual advances.

At this point, I wished Declan would do something as reckless as hit on me or shove his tongue down my throat in the elevator. Not so I could report him for it, but so that I could take him up on the offer and finally know what it was like to kiss him. At least then, I'd know that he felt the same way instead of wondering if he truly ever saw me as anything other than the person who sometimes answered his phones.

"Lily? Are you listening?"

I looked up to see Ellen, the object of my lust's actual assistant, hovering above my desk. "I'm sorry, what?"

She managed a small smile but looked annoyed at my obvious lack of respect. Ellen had been in our department the longest and was therefore the unofficial Matriarch of executive assistants. I knew she planned on working here until she couldn't work any longer. She'd informed me of that fact on more than one occasion, hinting that everyone else was temporary while she was as permanent as the statue at the front gates.

"I was saying that I have an appointment during lunch, so I'll be longer than an hour. Is that okay in terms of coverage?" she asked, and I nodded.

"Of course. It's fine," I said without a second thought because it was.

Part of our job requirements was to cover the other executive assistants' phones whenever they took a break or lunch. We coordinated with one another, scheduling around conflicts without any of the drama that usually accompanied a throng of women working together. It might have seemed old school, but the majority of the assistants in this particular department of Rockline Studios were women—with one exception.

That wasn't to say that the actual executives were all men because they weren't. There were two women running things here, but I wasn't assigned to either of them. And to tell you the truth, if Ellen decided one day to leave and never come back, I'd ask to switch from my boss to hers. And not just because I was in freaking love with the guy.

My boss was a complete dickhole with no qualms about acting like one. Marlo DeLong couldn't pick up his own phone and dial numbers if his life depended on it, yet he still insisted on treating me like he was somehow above me. Excuse me for not going to Harvard and into debt for the rest of my life for an education I could get somewhere else.

And unlike my typical douche bag of a boss, Declan Maguire never asked Ellen to fetch him coffee. He actually got his own.

When he'd introduced himself to me on my first day in our department kitchen, he'd poured *me* a cup, adding in one cream and one sugar—the way I liked it—before handing it over to me with a smile. Before I could ask him how he knew how I took it, he explained that he'd seen me make it that way earlier in the morning. It was a kindness he didn't have to show me, but he still had, and I thought I'd started falling for him right then and there.

I'd been falling ever since.

Declan never acted like he was above me—or anyone really—which was more than I could say for a lot of the other guys here. It was an ego thing. Men were typically ruled by it, but Declan never came off the same way. Maybe it was his thick Boston accent or the way he looked—all rogue, like he half didn't give a shit and half did. His dirty-blond hair always seemed to be mussed, the strands heading in different directions, but it suited him. On other men, it might look silly, out of place, or unprofessional, but on Declan, it just … *worked*. And don't get me started on those green eyes. They were things of beauty that starred in many of my dreams at night.

"Morning." The accent hit my ears, and I shook my head to glance up into the green eyes that haunted me.

He was devilishly handsome, and I could feel my pulse starting to race with his presence.

"Good morning," I said with a smile I wished I could stop. It was embarrassing how badly I wanted this man. And I swore he knew it. *How could he not?*

He walked away, and I admired his ass as he went before Ellen cleared her throat. I looked at her, and she shook her head at me with disapproval before following him into his office for their morning meeting. Even she knew how I felt about him. How mortifying!

"Lily!"

The sound of my voice being screamed into the hallway caused me to groan to myself, but I might have actually done it out loud.

"Today, Lily! Come on!"

I pushed up from my desk and headed toward my boss's office to begin another day of hell, being the assistant and verbal punching bag to the biggest asshole in our entire department.

IS IT WRONG TO HIT

A COWORKER?

⟡ DECLAN

SWORE TO God that if I heard Marlo shout Lily's name one more fucking time, I was going to head in there and punch him square in the jaw. At least that would get him to shut the hell up for a few seconds. The guy was a grade-A asshole. A complete tool who not only thought he was above his assistant, but the rest of us executive staff as well. He was your classic rich kid—you know the type. The one who had everything handed to him, including this job. Something about his dad being fraternity brothers with one of the bigwigs in the company.

I hated the guy.

And he had my girl.

"Declan." My assistant cleared her throat, and I refocused on her. "She's a strong woman."

Shaking my head, I pretended like I had no idea what she was talking about. "Excuse me?"

Ellen shifted uncomfortably in the chair across from my desk. I could tell that she was scared she'd crossed over some kind of invisible line.

"I just meant that Lily can handle Marlo. She's been doing it every day for over two years now."

I nodded. "I know. I just hate the way he screams out her name like he's too good to walk over to her desk or call her on the phone like a decent person."

"He is a special kind of asshole, if you don't mind me saying," Ellen said, and I started laughing.

I'd never heard her curse before. She always acted too refined and above all the nonsense we brought into the department on some days. Plus, she was old enough to be my mom, so I was a little afraid of her at times, to be honest. But the swearing, it was downright refreshing. I wondered what had taken her so long to let loose with me.

"He is, isn't he?" I asked with a smile, and she focused her attention back on the notebook in her hand.

We went over my schedule for the day, and she let me know that she would be taking an extra-long lunch and that

Lily would be covering my phones during that time. I tried to calm my heart down, but it got excited, just hearing that bit of news.

"Declan," Ellen started to say in the mom-like warning tone.

I braced myself for what was going to come. It was like I forgot that I was the boss here.

I cocked my head to the side and waited for Ellen to finish her thought, but she only stared at me, the wrinkles around her eyes more pronounced than usual, and I wondered for a second if she was okay, health-wise.

"Yes?" I pressed, and she blew out a quick breath.

"Just … be careful, is all." She knew. "You do remember what happened to Gustavo, don't you?"

Damn.

Ellen knew just the right punches to throw. It was like a brick to the guts.

Gustavo had fallen in love with his assistant. Normally, that might have just been a little sensitive in terms of the work environment if things went sour, but the bigger issue was that Gustavo's wife wasn't down with this love affair. She threatened to kill them both one night when they were working late. She actually came into the office, waving a handgun as she cried. It hadn't been pretty.

"Of course I remember Gustavo. But I'm not married, so there's no one to piss off."

"Andy," she countered, and I threw my head back and laughed to myself.

"Dammit, Ellen. I get it."

"Just don't want you going anywhere," she said before standing up from her chair as thoughts of Gustavo and Andy raced through my brain.

Andy had also dated an assistant at one time—not his. Things in the office were fine as long as they were happy and getting along, but the second their relationship started to fall apart, the entire department was affected. We were forced to take sides—the assistants on one and what felt like the rest of us on the other even if we weren't. Our days felt more like a war zone than an office with the battle lines sharply drawn.

It stopped production like you wouldn't believe. The assistants controlled our days. They had the power to make us miserable, by doing things like "accidentally" messing up meetings, transposing numbers for a dial-in, and "dropping" calls. It was hell. And all because one grown-ass adult couple had called it quits.

The assistant was eventually coerced into transferring departments, and we were all told to stop *shitting where we ate*. While the company couldn't legally impose a no-dating policy, it had become highly recommended that we *keep our dicks in our pants*—or so they'd implied in not so many words.

And while I'd never even been tempted to cross that line in all my years here, Lily St. Claire had started testing my resolve on day one.

She was so fucking beautiful when I saw her in the kitchen that I almost spit out my lukewarm coffee at the sight of her. I knew that didn't sound very attractive, but she'd caught me off guard with her long, dark hair and almond-shaped eyes looking up at me sweetly as I walked in. I watched as she added one cream and one sugar into her coffee before she smiled. *At me.*

Good Lord, I almost fell to my knees and started worshipping the ground she walked on based on those lips alone. It took every ounce of strength I had in my body not to take her in my arms and kiss the hell out of her. I walked away instead. Rushed out of the kitchen that morning to pull myself together and gather all the wits I'd apparently lost.

And I had no fucking idea why she'd made me so crazed. To put it simply, I was drawn to her, whether it was her energy, her vibe, or whatever you wanted to call it. Something about that woman had dragged me in. And I'd felt that draw every single day since. I'd thought the feeling might fade with time, but it never did. It was absolute torture to want someone this badly and be told to stay away from her.

Lily was smart too. Way too intelligent to be assisting that jackass, Marlo, even though brains were a requirement in order to work here. She should have been working her way up the ladder in another division altogether, not stuck here in a department that didn't allow for any growth. And that was the truth. Lily had nowhere to go. She could be an executive assistant or not work here. Which was fine for some people, like Ellen, who couldn't be happier in her job—thank God—but I could tell that Lily had been growing antsy lately. It was written all over her face. She wanted more than we could give her, and I didn't blame her. I would have craved more too by now.

"Wait!" I shouted at Ellen before she left my office completely.

Ellen walked back to the chair across from my desk once more and sat down. "Did we forget something?"

"Don't yell at me," I started to say, and she dropped her pen to the notebook with a thump. "But—"

"Declan," she scolded, and I put a hand up to stop her.

"I overheard Lily talking to you the other day about the

advertising department."

Ellen shifted in her seat and crossed her legs. "Mmhmm."

She wasn't going to make this easy on me.

"Can you tell me what she said? Does she want to work there? Is she looking to transfer?"

"You'd love that, wouldn't you?"

What do you think? Of course I'd love that. It would solve every problem. Then, I could finally fucking be a man and ask her out, make her fall head over heels in love with me, and have all my babies before she even realizes what's happened.

Those were all the things I thought in my head but didn't dare say out loud. Not to my assistant. And not to anyone.

"Ellen, why are you making this so hard on me?" I pouted. I actually fucking pouted to the woman who felt like a second mom to me, hoping she'd take mercy on my soul and give me all the details.

"Ugh," she groaned. "I have to admit, it's a little fun, torturing you," she said with a shrug, and I laughed again. Ellen was full of surprises today. "Okay. So, she is very interested in advertising in the theme park division. She checks the internal job board every day, but she's too scared to apply for anything again."

I stiffened in my chair, my posture instantly shifting. "What do you mean, again? And why is she scared?"

"Why do you think?"

Dammit. This woman was going to make me literally pull every morsel of information from her piece by piece. She refused to give me anything without begging.

"Ellen," I groaned, and she waved me off.

"Oh, you're no fun," she mockingly complained, and before I could continue my petulant whining, she continued, "You and I both know Marlo won't let her go. She applied to something a year ago, and he made sure to bury the application. Then, he called her in his office and told her if she wanted to leave this department, she'd have to quit the company altogether."

It took everything in me not to go all caveman and storm into Marlo's office and toss him out the damn window. It was only the second floor, so I knew he'd survive. I'd never been more tempted to provoke violence in my life. I had known he was an asshole, but this was another level of selfishness. The real reasons Marlo didn't want Lily to leave was because she was too good at her job and he liked looking at her ass. I'd seen him do it on more than one occasion. Like that motherfucker had even a sliver of a chance with my girl. Over my dead body.

I inhaled a long and what was supposed to be a calming breath through my nose, closed my eyes, and counted to ten before reopening them. "Ellen."

"I know, Declan. I told her to report him."

"She'd never do that," I said, shaking my head like I somehow knew her far more intimately than I really did.

"She loves working for Rockline. She doesn't want to have to leave."

My breathing had grown erratic, my chest tightening with each breath I took, which was supposed to be doing the opposite. "Thank you for telling me."

"Declan, don't do anything stupid," she warned, but I couldn't promise her that, so I said nothing. "This all happened a year ago. She doesn't seem as mad anymore."

Somehow, that made it all worse. That meant that a part of Lily had given up. You see, Rockline Studios didn't only create blockbuster movies for the masses to consume in theaters and online. We also owned publishing houses, record labels, radio stations, theme parks, cruise lines, television channels, and sports teams. If it was even remotely beneficial to the brand, we had our hands in it. And the minute it stopped making us money, we pulled out and sold it.

That was where our department, Planning and Development, entered the overall picture. We handled any and everything the company was looking to buy or sell across each division worldwide. Every person in our department, the assistants included, were handpicked, interviewed multiple times, and top-fucking-notch. The rest of the company knew it too. Our staff had a reputation of not only being the most cutthroat division on the entire studio lot, but also the most talented. To say we were feared wouldn't be an exaggeration. We had the power to shut down your department before you even knew it was in trouble.

But in that same vein was the CEO's overall vision that he demanded of us. He implored those of us who managed teams to really get to know everyone in them and forge an honest working relationship based on mutual respect and effective communication. He believed that if his employees were happy, they would do a good job. It was a simple concept really and part of the reason why I loved working here so much. I respected my boss and his outlook on running things.

I took it upon myself to have monthly check-in meetings with my direct staff, making sure they were mentally okay, still interested in being a part of my team, and I vetted any complaints or issues that might be growing underneath the surface. I completely understood that if, over time, the job they did lost its luster and another position within the company became more desirable. I'd personally helped my last junior director move over into one of the publishing houses when she told me that she had an interest in acquiring children's books.

The way I saw it was that it was my responsibility to help people reach their full potential, not keep them stuck doing something they would eventually hate and resent me for. I believed that we spent so much of our lives at work that we might as well love what we did while we were there.

But apparently, I was the only fucking one.

SOMETHING IS UP

⭐ LILY

ELLEN WALKED OUT of Declan's office with an odd expression on her face. It was truly unreadable. She gave me an even weirder look as she walked into our shared cubicle and sat down in front of her computer without saying a word to me. I watched her for a second or two before Marlo's phone started ringing and distracted me.

"Marlo DeLong's office. This is Lily. How can I help you?" I said into the line before a familiar voice greeted me.

"Lily, my favorite! How are you today?" the senior vice president of marketing bellowed into the line, the same way he always did whenever he called and I answered.

"I'm good, Mr. Callaway. How's New York this morning?"

"Freezing. I refuse to go outside. Tell me it's eighty degrees in California, and I'm hanging up the phone," he teased, and I laughed to myself before a shadow creeped over me and stopped.

Glancing up, I saw Marlo standing there, his arms crossed and a scowl on his face.

"Who is that?" he whispered harshly, and I covered the mouthpiece with my palm before whispering back the answer.

Marlo thrust his finger in the air, pointing toward his office as he stomped away—a silent demand that I get off the line and transfer the call. He hated that I *chit-chatted*, as he liked to say, with anyone who was calling for him.

"It's not. It's pretty cold here too," I lied because it wasn't cold.

There wasn't even a chill in the air even though it was late December and there should have been. California's weather was weird. It was so close to the holidays, but it felt nothing like it outside. Unless snowmen built out of sand and six-foot surfing waves at the beach felt like Christmas to you.

"You're lying," he called me out with a gruff laugh. "I like it."

"Mr. DeLong is waiting, so I'd better put you through," I said before placing the call on hold, the line flashing. Before I could alert Marlo to Mr. Callaway's waiting, he picked it up.

I was going to pay for that later with a stern talking-to or a reminder about my role in the company versus Marlo's. I never understood why he didn't see my being friendly to his associates as a good thing. The people who called for him enjoyed talking to me first. I was a reflection on him. And they all loved me. So, how was that so bad?

"He's going to blow a gasket one of these days," Ellen said, and I turned to look at her, resignation in my eyes.

"I know. He hates me," I said because I was truly starting to believe that he did.

If Marlo actually liked me, he would treat me nicer. But he didn't. And he never had.

I'd tried to transfer into another department once last year, but he'd found out about it and buried my application, letting me know that I hadn't worked here long enough to warrant a transfer. Something about paying my dues and if I wanted to go somewhere else, then maybe I should quit the company altogether.

I'd never felt more dejected before in the workplace, but I sucked it up, determined to figure out a way to leave without Marlo finding out about it. I could have quit, like he'd suggested, and found a new job, but I loved working here. Rockline Studios was exciting with movies and television shows being filmed outside and celebrities eating in the commissary—you never knew who you might run into. And the perks were unlike anything I'd ever experienced before—lavish parties, theme park passes, and Hollywood movie premieres.

To put it mildly, I never wanted to work anywhere else again.

Not to mention the fact that Dreamboat Declan was here. And if I was forced to stay put in this particular position, at least I got to see him every day. He saved me, and he didn't even know it. Declan made my personal hell tolerable. Heck, he made me want to tolerate it.

Whenever I considered transferring out of P&D, the thought of never seeing Declan again sent me spiraling into some sort of schoolgirl depression. The studio lot was massive, and the separate divisions had very little interaction on a day-to-day basis. There was a very large chance that when I left here, I'd never run into or see Declan again.

I couldn't even stomach the idea of it. I didn't care how "pathetic" that might make me. In my head, Declan was all mine—to do with what and how I pleased and as often as I craved him. Every freaking day, I thanked God that he didn't have a girlfriend. How he'd avoided being snagged up, I had no idea, but trust me, I wasn't complaining.

"I don't think he hates you." Ellen's voice busted into my thoughts, and I'd forgotten that we were even having a conversation.

"Well, he definitely doesn't like me," I argued, and she made a sour face.

"I think he's just miserable. He takes it out on you."

I tossed my hands in the air like I was holding a pair of pom-poms. "Yay me."

"I shouldn't tell you this but," she started to say before thinking better of it and shutting her mouth. "Oh, never mind. Sorry."

Who does that? You can't just start to tell a person something and then take it back!

"No! What were you going to say?" I asked—pleaded really—hoping that it had something to do with Declan professing his undying love for me and her knowledge of said love.

"It was nothing. Slip of the tongue," she said innocently, and I scowled at her in response.

There was no amount of whining or cajoling that was going to get Ellen to spill the tea on something she had no intention of telling me, so I didn't even bother trying.

"Fine." I turned back to face my computer and began responding to the emails that had piled up in the last fifteen minutes.

Being an executive assistant was relentless. The job literally never ended. Just when you thought you might get a reprieve, the phone started to ring, the emails began piling back up, or a last-minute meeting needed to be coordinated with at least ten people—all of them in different time zones. Not to mention, the constant building of slide shows. P&D lived for PowerPoint presentations. Every single potential acquisition required one. Either showing why it was beneficial for us to try to purchase or why it wasn't.

"Are you coming to the party?" Ellen asked, once again diverting my attention in her direction.

"Yes. Of course. Are you?" I said because I always went to Rockline Studios New Year's Eve parties, and I assumed that everyone else did, too, even if I never saw them there.

"I'll be there," she said with a beaming smile that I rarely saw.

Most normal companies held their holiday parties either well before or around Christmas but not us. No, nothing at Rockline Studios was typical by any means. Or boring. Employees weren't required to attend the yearly bash, but if we did, we were guaranteed to be at the most exclusive New Year's Eve parties in all of Los Angeles.

I had to admit that the party was genius from a

marketing perspective, so whoever had originally thought it up deserved a freaking medal. Or a brownie. It was an invite-only, VIP affair that many clamored to get a ticket to. They placed requests on social media sites, bartered and begged their agents to do whatever was necessary to get them in.

A-list actors and actresses were always invited, and the majority of them attended, only opting out if they weren't in town. There was no other acceptable reason not to come. No one in the entertainment industry wanted to miss out on the networking opportunities that the studio was famously notorious for breeding. Many Oscar-nominated movies were conceived during the Rockline New Year's Eve bash.

Rockline was one of the largest movie studios in LA, and each year on New Year's Eve, our enormous production stages were turned into a themed party, complete with fully constructed movie sets and realistic props. Last year, a lake that you could take an actual boat ride on had sat in the middle of what was supposed to be Central Park. I'd never been to New York before, but I'd assumed the party was an exact replica.

This year, the theme was the *Roaring Twenties*—after our biggest box office–grossing hit. I couldn't wait to see how it would be decorated. Not to mention the fact that I was absolutely in love with the dress I'd bought for it, complete with fringe and a feather headband.

"Are you bringing your husband?"

"You think Henry would let me go to that party by myself? Not a chance," she said, and I laughed. "Plus, if I saw Scarlett Johansson without him, he might divorce me."

"He's a big ScarJo fan, huh?"

She groaned. "The biggest. It's okay though because I'd leave him in a heartbeat for Kevin Costner."

I started laughing. "Good to know."

"What about you?"

I narrowed my eyes. "What about me, what?"

"Which celebrity do you have a thing for?" she asked, and I pursed my lips together as I thought about the question. "Oh, come on, Lily. It can't be that hard. Who was the first man that came to your head?"

Declan.

Declan was my celebrity crush. *Be quiet.* I knew he wasn't a celebrity, but there was no room in my heart for any more unrequited love affairs.

But I couldn't tell her that.

"I don't know. I mean, they're all good-looking. But they're so much shorter and skinnier than they look on TV."

"Isn't that the truth?" she said right as the phone rang,

and she sprang into action to answer it.

It absolutely was the truth. All the guys in Hollywood looked like they were over six feet tall and super beefy whenever you saw them next to their leading ladies. But the thing was, the girls were all so teeny-tiny that it didn't take much for the guys to appear bigger than they were. For example, if a girl was only five foot two, then even a guy at five foot seven would look like he towered over her on the big screen. And we all knew that five foot seven wasn't very tall for a dude.

Sorry, guys.

It was a weird reality whenever I saw the actors in person at these parties or walking around on the lot. They tended to be fairly short. Super skinny. And they almost always had softer, suppler skin than I did. The majority of the actors in this town were way prettier than I was.

I liked a manlier man. A guy who actually did tower over me. And one with muscles that included some actual body fat on the percentage scale. I wasn't into stick-thin pretty boys. Men like Declan were more my type. Mussed-up hair, chiseled jaw with scruff that begged to be played with. Thighs that were thicker than mine with what hopefully led to a similar appendage inside his pants.

No sooner was I sketching Declan's naked form in my

mind than he appeared in front of Ellen's desk, talking in a low voice. I glanced at him, steeling my gaze so that I wouldn't give away all the dirty things I'd just been thinking. In return, he gave me a forced smile before walking away, and Ellen looked at me like I had a neon sign over my head, displaying all of my fantasies in detail.

"Did I do something wrong?" I asked.

Ellen blew out a breath and shook her head. "Not that I'm aware of."

"Is Declan mad at me?" I pushed, knowing that I was treading on dangerous ground.

"Why would my boss be mad at you?"

"I don't know. That's why I'm asking."

She threw her hands up in the air. "I'm not getting in the middle of you two."

She's not doing what? Getting in the middle of us? I wish there were something to get in the middle of.

"What do you mean?" I asked in shock because the last time I'd checked, my crush was pretty one-sided.

"Like I said"—she put her hands up again—"not getting in the middle of it."

"Ellen"—I rolled my office chair into the middle of our shared cubicle, my curiosity piqued—"you worked here when there was all that dating drama before, right?"

Ellen's face damn near lit up. I'd never seen her look more excited as she scooted her chair closer to me. "I was. You don't know, do you?"

I shook my head and listened closely as she told me two stories. One about a guy named Andy and the other about a man named Gustavo. I'd heard bits and pieces of what had happened, but they were nothing in comparison to what Ellen shared. She knew every single thing, and she explained it all to me, in excruciating and graphic detail before mentioning that Declan had been working here as well at the time of both incidents.

If there had been an ember burning inside of me for Declan, Ellen doused it with waves of water, extinguishing it before it had the chance to grow into a flame. There was no way, after learning what I just had, that Declan would ever cross that line with me—or anyone. He was too honest and too good at his job to risk losing it.

I couldn't even say that I blamed him. After hearing those two stories, I wasn't sure I would chance it either.

STOP BEING A PUSSY

✪ DECLAN

L *ILY ST. CLAIRE.*

Lily St. Claire.

LILY ST. CLAIRE.

The fact that she had burrowed herself into my thoughts and wouldn't get the fuck out was beyond a problem at this point. And it'd only gotten worse with time. When I was rubbing one out in the shower or tugging my cock all alone in bed, it was Lily who made me come. It was her face I saw, her voice I heard, and her body I imagined fucking.

I wanted to grab her in my arms, throw her up against the wall, and pleasure her until she couldn't take it a second longer as her lips screamed out my name for all the world to hear. But Ellen's warning rolled around in my head, refusing to leave. Anytime I got close to saying *fuck it all* and asking her to the New Year's Eve party, I remembered what had happened to Andy. Office romances were always tricky regardless of where you worked, but this seemed even more complicated somehow. Maybe because it was *my* office and the romance was supposed to be *mine*.

I was a grown man, for fuck's sake. I should be able to ask out whoever I wanted, but I knew that wasn't really the case. It was absolute bullshit that a personal relationship between two consenting adults had been able to wreak such havoc on all of our professional lives, but it had. And I was still scarred from the damage; even without Ellen's reminder, the fallout lingered.

Do you have any idea how long and torturous two years felt to a person when he'd been lying in wait? Because that was what I'd been doing … *waiting*. Biding my time, hoping something might change—that she might transfer or quit—or that I'd finally figure out a way to make this work without anyone knowing. The worst that could happen was if Lily dashed all my hopes and told me she had a boyfriend.

It would kill me, but it would probably be for the best since neither one of us was clearly leaving P&D.

I meant it though.

I would die of jealousy.

And I would fucking deserve it because I'd let her go.

The past two years, I'd been letting her go. Watching her walk away. Doing every damn thing, except the one I actually longed to.

Make.

Her.

Mine.

Standing up from my desk, I knew that my assistant was heading out to an appointment, so I'd have to interact with Lily. It was like I enjoyed the torture or something. I stepped toward their cubicle, noticing that Ellen's was empty.

"Lily," I said her name softer than I'd meant to, and she didn't hear me at first. "Lily," I said again, only louder this time.

She turned around, her eyes widening at first before her expression cooled. "Hi. Do you need me to order you lunch?"

I completely forgot why I'd walked out there in the first place. Did she have any idea how stunning she was? She rendered me fucking clueless with just one look.

"Declan?"

Shit.

"Sorry," I said, attempting to pull myself together but it was a struggle. "I, um"—I cleared my throat—"wanted to let you know that I'm expecting a call from overseas. It's really important."

I watched as she nodded her head, her dark hair flowing with the movement. "Ellen let me know. I'll make sure to find you," she said with a grin before adding, "Just don't go far."

Is she flirting? I wasn't sure.

"I mean, I won't be able to reach you if you leave without telling me. And then they'll ask you to call back, and by the time you do, they'll be on another call. You know how it is," she overexplained as her cheeks turned pink.

I thought she was as flustered as I was.

"No, right." I was a bumbling fool all of a sudden. "I'll let you know if I leave the building," I started before her smile turned into a frown. "But I won't. I mean, I won't leave the building when I'm expecting a call from London. That would be dumb. Right?"

A nervous laugh escaped me, and she looked right into my eyes and held them.

Holy shit, what the hell is wrong with me?

"Get away from my assistant, Declan."

Marlo's nasally voice hit my ears, and I turned to see him stalking down the hall in my direction. His presence snapped me out of my teen-like trance.

"Lily's my assistant, too, right now."

"Well, she was mine first."

"We share her," I said, choking on the word. The last thing in the world I wanted to do was even mention the word *share* and *Lily* in the same sentence.

"We don't," he countered.

Lily's head ping-ponged back and forth between me and Marlo as we acted like two idiots, fighting over the last candy bar in a store.

"Guys!" Lily yelled, and we both stopped measuring our dicks for two seconds to stare at her. "I can handle both of your phones. I do it every single day," she said, completely calm and composed. "Declan, I'll make sure to find you as soon as London calls. And, Marlo, what can I do for you?"

That was it. I was being dismissed. She wasn't even looking at me anymore, her focus solely on her true boss as she waited for his response. I tucked my tail between my legs and walked off, throwing one last glance behind me. I saw the shit-eating grin on Marlo's face, like he'd won some sort of battle here today when that couldn't have been further from the truth.

He hadn't won anything.

I'd make sure of it.

THAT WAS WEIRD

⭐ LILY

'D NEVER SEEN Declan act so … *bizarre*. There had been something else he had to say, or confess, or ask me—I could see it in his eyes—but Marlo had walked up and ruined everything between us. If I didn't know any better, I'd think he had done it on purpose.

Not that my boss had a thing for me. It really wasn't like that. Marlo was simply the type of guy who enjoyed possessing things … and *people*. He made sure everyone knew what belonged to him, and he acted like I was part of his property, figuratively pissing all over me every chance he got.

Declan definitely didn't like it.

And I loved knowing that it bothered him. Even if I had no idea what it all meant, it still felt good. If things were reversed and Declan's assistant acted like she owned him,

I'd come unglued too. It would drive me crazy—and not in a good way.

Shaking my head, I reminded myself about the relationship drama Ellen had filled me in on earlier. Basically, none of it mattered—not the way I felt about Declan, not the way Declan felt about me (if anything)—because there was no way in hell he'd ever act on it. I needed to get the thoughts of him out of my head.

It was a good thing that Christmas was right around the corner. The distance would be helpful.

At least, that was what I tried to convince myself of … right up until the day before break started and Declan stalked up to my desk, leaned toward me, and whispered, "See you at the party," before walking away without waiting for a response.

I turned to look at Ellen, who was watching with rapt attention, her eyebrows raised.

"What was that all about?" she asked with disapproval in her voice.

I shrugged. "Nothing," I answered because that was what it had been, right? Nothing.

CHRISTMAS CAME AND went, and I'd spent every single

morning of my break from the office sleeping in with the exception of Christmas morning when I had to be at my parents' house in the Valley at the ass crack of dawn. There were few things more blissful than sleep, and I never got enough of it, even on weekends. The week off at Rockline Studios between the two holidays was the one time of year that I relished in snoozing past ten a.m. I refused to feel guilty about it, loving the way my covers felt while tucked up around my chin, my body surrounded by pillows, my lustful dreams keeping me warm.

I sat out on my balcony for hours, the warm sun tickling my toes as I read on my Kindle. This time off was filled with all the things I never seemed to have enough time to do. Reading, catching extra z's, and watching all the shows I had piling up on my DVR with a pint—or three—of ice cream.

I loved my alone time—something most people, my little sister included, never seemed to understand. She insisted that I hit the bars and clubs in Hollywood with her every night, texting me like crazy, but the last thing I wanted to do was go out and meet shitty, egotistical, self-absorbed guys that meant nothing and went nowhere. Been there, done that. More than a few times over, if I was being honest. It was such a waste of time, and I had zero interest in any of it anymore.

That was when I had known I was getting old. Ha! Most of my friends were already married and had at least one kid, some with another on the way. I was technically behind, but I never felt it. If there was such a thing as a biological clock, mine had definitely stopped ticking. Or maybe it hadn't started yet. All I knew was that I wasn't the kind of person who rushed into things, especially marriage and babies. I'd just found my dream company to work for; I was content with focusing on that aspect of my life.

Speaking of, the most annoying thing was how much I still seemed to think about Declan. I was supposed to be giving myself a break from him, but it'd proven to be impossible. My mind was definitely not on board with Operation Get Over the D. And I absolutely meant both versions—Declan and his dick. Not that I had any idea what it looked like, but in my imagination, it was perfection, all thick and filling and basically made for me.

Even the fictional boyfriends in my books didn't compare to him. I found myself making mental notes on what the guys in my stories said and did versus what Declan had said and done, and he won every single time. Mostly because Declan was real.

And I would get to see him tonight. In theory.

When it came to the Rockline New Year's Eve party, you were lucky to run into any of your coworkers at all if you didn't come to the bash with them. The event was massive, overwhelming, and exciting. But finding people you knew was nearly impossible. I always thought that it was an odd way to show appreciation for all of your staff's hard work over the year, but then again, that was what the year-end bonuses were for. If I had to choose between the two, I'd rather have the extra money ten times out of ten. The money was helpful. The parties were just … the most talked about event of the year.

My phone pinged out with a text message, and to my surprise, it was from Ellen and not my little sister. We had never once talked or texted during the holiday break before, so this was a first.

"You're still coming to the party tonight?" she asked, and I found the question a little odd as I stared at the words on my phone.

"Of course. Why?"

"My husband is sick. I was debating on whether or not to stay home or go without him."

Ohh. I wasn't sure how to respond.

As much as I liked Ellen, I really hadn't planned on spending the night of LA's biggest party by her side. Just the thought of it sort of depressed me. Not that Ellen wasn't a wonderful coworker, but she didn't really strike me as *fun*.

Before I could think of what to say or how to respond, another text came through.

"I'm going to stay home with him. If he feels better, we'll both be there. Have fun."

I felt a little bad for her but not enough to try to convince her to ditch her husband and hang out with me instead, so I sent her a text that said, "That sucks, but you're a really good wife. Hope he feels better."

I wasn't sure what else I was supposed to say, so I hoped that was enough and that it hadn't come across as rude. When she never responded, I checked the clock on the wall and noted that I still had a couple of hours before I needed to start getting ready.

Keeping my butt firmly planted on my chair outside, I turned my Kindle back on and continued reading.

MY CAR WAS parked in the overflow lot as I walked by myself toward the stage where the party was being held. I thought I'd arrived fairly early, but it was already a madhouse with crowds that rivaled the entrance to Disneyland on a summer day. There were people in front of and behind me, all dressed to the nines, but I didn't immediately recognize anyone. And to be honest, I was too embarrassed to outright stare or gawk just to see if I was surrounded by movie stars or not.

The evening air held a chill, and there was a line to get in. I should have grabbed some sort of jacket, but I'd talked myself out of it before I left, deciding that I'd only be outside briefly and it wasn't worth waiting in line at the coat check. Wrapping my arms around my middle, I squeezed myself, hoping I didn't look anywhere near as cold as I felt as anxiety ripped through me. I was feeling so anxious for no reason at all that I could place as I gave my name to the man guarding the entrance and showed him my studio identification card before shoving it back into my clutch.

"Enjoy your evening, Miss St. Claire," he said as I stepped through the steel door and into an absolutely breath-stealing wonderland.

My jaw dropped open as I took in the scene in front of me, my body instantly stopping its forward motion, as if I'd stepped in quicksand, my legs refusing to move. The previously empty space had been transformed into not only the main character's mansion from the *Roaring Twenties* movie hit, but the outdoor grounds as well. A winding grand staircase took center stage as far up as the eye could see. I was pretty sure it was the one used in the actual film. A film I'd seen no less than ten times already. I was sort of obsessed with it.

There was a large lawn with perfectly manicured hedges that directed the traffic without being obvious. And the flowers … holy shit, there were so many flowers—in large pots, in vases, on the ground. Multiple trees with mini lights hanging on them illuminated the space between the mansion and the cottage, interspersed with benches for sitting, and there were even old-fashioned cars that you could take pictures in. Everything was so opulent and stunning. It was no wonder that everyone wanted to come to this party; even regular people like myself felt like a star.

Once I convinced my legs to start moving again, I made my way to the spiral staircase and grabbed the railing with one hand. I stepped carefully, doing my best not to fall and embarrass the hell out of myself as I made my way up, up, up. When I reached the top, it opened up into what was supposed to be a hallway that led to the bedrooms, but they actually led nowhere. This could easily double as an additional dance floor later on … as long as no one plummeted to their death.

The candlelight glowed all around me as I let my head fall back, forgetting that I wasn't really in someone's house for a moment. The normal steel beams that ran across the ceiling had been transformed to look like the night sky. There was no end to the stage, only an everlasting galaxy with a full moon that gave off a real-life glow, accompanied by a plethora of stars that you could never, ever see in Los Angeles.

This company was truly something else. They'd pulled out all the stops, spared no expense, and turned an empty warehouse into a mystical wonderland.

No sooner had a small smile crept across my face than I spotted a shooting star streaking across the fake sky. I watched in silent awe, my mind knowing that it wasn't truly real, but my imagination buying into everything this night was selling. Call me silly, but I wanted to make a wish.

It was New Year's Eve, and that meant the start of a new beginning and a new year. Anything and everything felt possible. It was like hitting the reset button on your life or starting over, if that was what you needed to do. New Year's Eve always felt magical to me, like nothing was out of reach if you only believed hard enough—and made a glitter-filled vision board. With that mind-set, I refused to let even a fake falling star go to waste.

So, I closed my eyes and made that wish.

I wished that Declan would let his guard down and have

his way with me … even if it was just for one night. I tried to convince myself that a single evening was all I needed to get him out of my system. That maybe if I had a taste of Declan Maguire, that would be enough. One taste, and I'd be able to walk away, forget it ever happened, and put him in the back of my mind forever.

I laughed out loud at the thought. It was a downright lie, but I bought into it because it was the only way this whole thing seemed even remotely plausible.

Chills raced through my body as a horrible thought entered my mind. *What if he's not alone?*

Declan had come to the parties the last two years without a date—I'd found out afterward—but what if he had a girlfriend I didn't know about and he brought her this year?

No. I refused to think negatively.

In my fiction-filled head, Declan was single, ready to mingle, and wanted me just as badly as I wanted him. So, here I was, standing at the top of a winding staircase, watching fake stars glide across an even faker sky, wishing for a boy to love me like some teenager with a dream.

PARTY OF THE YEAR

✧ DECLAN

C LUTCHING THE WATERED-DOWN whiskey drink in my hand, I looked around at the massive party. I was half in awe over the decor that the set and design team had clearly outdone themselves on while the rest of me wondered where the hell Lily St. Claire might be. I fucking loved our parties, but it did make trying to find someone you were looking for extremely difficult.

Sometimes, I could go the entire night without seeing a single person from my department. It sort of defeated the purpose of having a company party, if you asked me. But then again, no one was … asking me, that was.

I'd gone back home to Boston for the holidays, like I did each year. It was cold as balls, and my family all teased me about having gone "Californian" on them. To be honest, I had turned into a bit of a pussy about the snow now that I

50

didn't live in it anymore. But who the hell wanted to live in freezing temperatures when you didn't have to?

Not me.

As I was the oldest Maguire boy, they grilled me about girls and all the celebrities I'd met over the years, wondering why I hadn't snatched one up yet. It was hilarious, the way people outside of Hollywood perceived it. Like I should have made my way through all the available actresses by now or something equally as insane.

But mostly, my mom just wanted to know when I'd finally bring home someone special. She wanted me to find love and was concerned that I had moved someplace that made it infinitely difficult. I spent the rest of the time talking about Lily. As we sat around the dinner table, they analyzed my feelings and listened to my apprehension about dating someone in the workplace. It felt like a freaking intervention, but my family had this innate ability to drag out even the most uncomfortable of feelings from one another. We did it on the regular. And it always helped.

After listening to me go on and on about her for days, they encouraged me to go for it.

They'd all asked me, "What's the worst thing that could happen?"

Well, the worst thing was that I'd lose my job, be forced

out of the entertainment industry altogether, and never work in this town again.

Hey, we were talking about worst-case scenarios here.

And that was basically it. When my parents had told me that the right girl was worth the risk and that having a job you loved with no one to share it with wasn't living at all, it was the gentle push that I'd required.

I knew they were right. The only thing that held me back from asking Lily out was fear. I was scared of the potential consequences. And I was not the kind of guy who was scared of shit.

Looking down at my cell phone, I noticed a text from my mom. She wished me good luck, reminded me to go for it, and then told me to send her pictures of us kissing at midnight because she knew I wouldn't let her down.

Jesus, Mother, no pressure or anything.

Swirling the melting ice in my old-fashioned, I looked toward the ceiling, my mind still impressed over what our set department could create. If I hadn't known any better, I would have bet money that I was standing outside, in a stunning courtyard garden, looking up at the real night sky. It was incredible, the atmosphere that had been created here tonight. Inspiring even.

I watched as a single star danced across the ceiling,

mimicking a shooting star, and like a fool, I made a wish. I couldn't help it. When I had been a kid, my mom had always told me that falling stars were a gift you had to wish on, and I'd been doing exactly that ever since. Tonight was no different; made-up star or not, I wished that Lily St. Claire would finally look at me the way I looked at her. Give me a sign, a nod, the go-ahead glance to make all my fantasies come true.

Taking another swig of my watered-down drink, I winced before my eyes were pulled toward the sky once more but this time not quite as high. And I almost fucking choked as the liquid went down the wrong pipe. Lily stood at the top of a staircase, looking like a goddess.

She was a vision, and I couldn't stop staring. Her long, dark hair spilled around her shoulders and down to her breasts in subtle waves. It was normally stick straight in the office, but seeing it now with curls in it ignited something inside of me. I'd always wanted to wrap my hands in her hair, but now, I wanted to get all tangled up in it, see it splayed across my chest, my pillow, and my bed.

The red dress she wore hugged every single curve on her body that she usually hid at work underneath business attire. I had known she had a figure, but I'd had no idea how gorgeous her body really was. The dress left little to the imagination, and I hated thinking that someone else might be looking at her, thinking the same thoughts I was. Her body was a winding road map, and I wanted to drive all over it, intimately familiarizing myself with those curves and never fucking stopping.

Lily St. Claire was meant to be mine, and tonight, I'd make sure she knew it.

Downing the rest of my shitty drink for a little liquid courage, I shook my head to myself and decided that I would change everything. No more waiting around, being Mr. Nice Guy and pretending like these feelings I had for her didn't exist. Tonight, I'd tell Lily everything I'd been too chickenshit to tell her the past two years.

Tonight, I'd get my girl.

Company rules and consequences be damned.

My family would be so proud.

WAIT, WHAT?

✧ LILY

I LIKED STANDING on the staircase, navigating the world below from far above it. It felt more peaceful than trying to actually walk through the massive crowd downstairs, especially when you didn't know most of the people there, which I definitely didn't.

If I was on the ground floor right now, I'd most likely be standing there alone, feeling like a bit of an idiot for no reason other than it was always weird, being at a party filled with strangers instead of friends. Nothing felt more uncomfortable or awkward than feeling like everyone was staring at you while you tried desperately to find one person you recognized.

I'd made the mistake of texting a couple of the other assistants that I would meet them inside instead of driving together, but so far, I hadn't seen a single one of them. And to make matters more difficult, I'd left my cell phone in my car, so I couldn't even send them a text. The last thing I was going to do was trek back out there in the cold and wait in line to get back in again.

Peering down at the overly crowded floor once more, I eyed everyone, trying my best to tell them apart from a distance. That was when I saw him. I almost couldn't believe it. Declan was looking up—hopefully at me—and my heart was beating so hard that I swore you could see it pounding right through my dress.

My eyes locked on to his as he stood there, staring, a small smirk playing on his lips, and I knew he was staring at me too. I smiled in return and watched as he ducked through the crowd and disappeared from my view, and disappointment coursed through me.

One look at me, and he left?

So much for my wish, I thought to myself until the sound of footsteps pounding against the wood flooring averted my attention.

I turned around to see Declan climbing the stairs two at a time, making his way toward me, a drink in his hand. I bit my bottom lip to stop myself from smiling like a fool, but he looked so determined, and it turned me the hell on. As he approached, I clenched my legs together, knowing this was technically a company party and he was my superior but, my God, Declan Maguire looked damn good in a black suit and tie.

"Lily." He reached for my hand and planted a kiss on top of it. It should have been awkward or weird, but it felt romantic and gentlemanly. Almost like we were part of the movie they filmed on these sets, tossed back in time to when men acted with class. Or at least, they pretended to.

"Hi." I smiled in return, unable to hide the fact that I loved his touch, craved it even more, and was most likely never going to wash my hand again.

His eyes didn't look away from me as he spoke, the way they normally did when we talked in the office. This time, they peered right into me … with interest maybe? I couldn't be certain. There was a good chance that my hopeful heart was talking, trying to convince me that my wish was coming true.

"You look beautiful."

He stepped closer, his body mere inches from mine, and I struggled to catch my breath.

"So damn beautiful," he said again, and I did my best to swallow oxygen in his presence, but it was a challenge.

"So do you," I said before practically choking on my idiotic response. "I mean, you look gorgeous. Shit.

Handsome. Shit. I'm sorry I keep saying *shit*. Don't fire me." I turned away from him, feeling like a complete lunatic as his deep laughter rang in my ears. My face flamed with my embarrassment.

"Lily, look at me," he spoke sternly, his hand on my arm as he maneuvered me back around.

My eyes met his once again, and I wanted to swoon out loud, simply from the way that look was making me feel. Like I was floating on air, weightless, tethered to him by some invisible string I couldn't see.

"How would I get to see you every day if I had you fired?"

Wait, what?

I coughed a little as my breath caught in my throat, and I tried desperately to formulate a non-mortifying response. "Are you saying you like seeing me every day?"

He grinned, the five o'clock shadow on his face begging me to run my fingers across it. "I love seeing you every day."

Biting down on my lower lip, I muttered, my question barely skirting past my lips, "Really?"

He took another small step closer to me, his chest well within reach, and my brain fought against my hands, convincing them to stay put at my sides instead of reaching out for him and touching him the way I'd always wanted to.

"Yes, really," he said, his voice husky, the very timbre of it turning me on in every way possible.

Chills raced down my spine. My pussy woke up from whatever trance she'd been in. Every nerve inside my body shot to life as his head moved toward mine, and my heart stopped beating in anticipation.

I held my breath. Was Declan Maguire going to kiss me right now? Oh my God, how long I'd wanted this to happen. How many times had I fantasized about having those lips on mine? My wish was coming true, and I'd never wanted anything more.

"Declan!" the sound of his name being shouted pulled our attention away from each other at the exact same time, and I swore my vagina started weeping in response.

I'd completely forgotten that anyone else was even in the room. I turned to scan the area around us, searching for the source, as the shouting continued, the voice all too familiar, and ruining the moment.

"Dammit. Asshole," Declan said before he turned toward the commotion on the ground level.

I got nervous that we'd been caught in a bit of a compromising position and that Declan might get in trouble. Could everyone see us clearly from down below? I wasn't really sure as Declan stared toward where Marlo—my boss and his coworker—stood, still yelling as he pointed up at the two of us. His gelled black hair was way too long and falling into his eyes instead of staying plastered in place on his head, like I knew he meant for it to do. I'd never run into anyone at these things, and this was the one time I'd not only seen Declan, but my boss as well.

It got even better. Next to Marlo stood the CEO of the entire company, Richard, staring up at us as well through his standard wire-rimmed glasses. Rumor was that he didn't even need them and they were made of plain glass, but no one really knew for sure. All I knew was that I'd never seen him without them on. And now, he was watching us, his gaze intent.

I groaned out loud, stepping back a few paces to remove myself from their direct line of sight. Declan moved toward me, seemingly instinctively, closing the space I'd just created, and I prayed that we were at least hidden by shadows or the candlelight.

"I'll be right back, Lily. Don't move." He reached for my hand and kissed the top of it once more. "I mean it. Don't go anywhere. We're not finished here."

I fought back the excited nerves that coursed through me but didn't respond to his request or even say anything at all in response. I didn't think I could have spoken in that moment if you paid me.

Declan stopped walking away. "Lily?"

Swallowing hard, I muttered, "Yes?"

"I mean it. Don't leave," he demanded again before stalking back toward me, his shoulders squared, his tux looking like it had been made for him as he focused solely on me.

He reached for my chin, tilting it up to meet his green eyes before planting a soft kiss on my cheek as my eyes closed in response. I swore I moaned out loud.

"I want to finish what we started," he said with a devilish smile that no woman on earth could resist. "Okay?"

"Okay," I agreed as I watched him walk away, a little more swagger in his step than he'd had before.

I wondered what it was exactly that we'd just started and prayed to the heavens that it was only the beginning of something beautiful. If Declan Maguire wanted to give me attention, flirt with me, or tell me he liked seeing me every day, I'd sure as hell take it. And if he wanted to finish whatever we'd started, I was definitely game for one night—or a thousand.

It felt like a million hours had passed while I waited for him to return to me. Stepping out of the shadows, I glanced down at the floor. The three of them no longer stood where they once had, and I had no idea where Declan had gone or if he was even coming back even though he'd said he would. The CEO had summoned him, and so, really, he hadn't had an option.

I continued to scan the area below, looking in vain for Declan when my eyes fell on a pair seemingly staring back at me.

Colton Adams.

The Colton Adams was staring up at me—or at least, it looked like he was. The theme for tonight's party had been built around the movie that Colton had starred in. The movie he'd won an Oscar for. His lips formed a perfect Hollywood smile before he pointed at me and signaled for me to come down. I looked behind me to make sure he wasn't talking to someone else, and I noticed him laugh in response. When I jabbed a finger at my chest to make sure, Colton nodded once and waved me down again. I gave him a little shrug and headed toward the long, winding staircase, wondering what the hell I was about to walk into and what Colton Adams could possibly want with me.

Stepping carefully, I made my way toward the star of the evening and wondered how my night could get any weirder.

LEAVING LILY

DECLAN

S^{*HIT*}.

S*HIT*.

The last thing I'd wanted to do was leave Lily's side, but when the CEO of the damn studio summoned you with your jackass coworker, you went running. And run I did, away from the most beautiful woman in the whole entire room. She clearly had no idea I'd just left my heart in her hands, hoping like hell she wouldn't drop it or toss it over the railing to the floor for someone to step on.

The look in her eyes had told me she was counting down the seconds until my lips finally touched hers, and I wanted to do a little dance just from learning that fact. Lily St. Claire wanted me to kiss her. And I was damn straight going to do it. Right after I sucked it up, played the game, and got this over with.

When I reached the last step, the two men were waiting

for me, sly grins on both their faces.

"Richard. Marlo," I said, giving them each a firm handshake before sneaking a glance up to where I had just stood with Lily.

She hadn't come down the stairs behind me, but I couldn't see her from my current vantage point, and I wondered if Marlo had been able to see her at all when he cockblocked me. It was a damn shame that she was hiding in the shadows because that woman was a sight to behold, an absolute vision. Then again, I liked the fact that no one else could lose their mind just from looking at her. She was mine to ogle, to daydream about, to make my move on once and for all.

"Great job, Declan. I wasn't sure we'd come out on top for that one" he said, and I nodded in agreement.

"It got a little aggressive there toward the end," I added for emphasis.

"But we won." He clapped an arm on my back. "We always do."

Richard continued to carry on about work, congratulating me on the deal I had just negotiated to purchase a new network to add to our ever-growing franchise. I didn't want to talk about work tonight, but I obliged him because that was what you did when you worked for someone else—you adjusted your needs and wants to meet theirs.

I refused to call it ass-kissing, which was more than likely what it was, but I'd never seen myself as that type of guy, and I didn't want to start now. I was a rock-star negotiator, great at my fucking job, and someone else could have easily blown the deal.

"So, I saw you upstairs with my assistant, Declan," Marlo said a little too loudly in my direction.

I guessed that answered that question—he could see us both from his position on the floor.

I looked carefully at Richard, who was thankfully shaking hands with someone I didn't know, his attention diverted, and I gave a tight-lipped nod toward Marlo, not wanting to broach that topic with him—or anyone else for that matter.

"So, boys, celebratory shots?" Richard was back in the fold before Marlo could get another word out or question me more.

"Really?" I let out a short laugh, remembering the last time he'd asked us to do shots with him.

It had been at an after-party for a movie premiere, and he made us do sake bombs until one of us yelled truce. Needless to say, the old man had won, and he never let us forget it. How the hell he had drunk all of us young guys under the table that night I never figured out, but I hoped we wouldn't be having a repeat performance.

I'd had to call an Uber to take me home, and I spent the entire next day with my head in the toilet, wishing for death to come and take me. When Monday morning had finally rolled around, the big man had teased me relentlessly, calling me a rookie and shit. I didn't need that again.

"You got a problem doing shots with your boss, Declan?" Richard teased with a smirk as he adjusted his glasses.

I cleared my throat. "Not at all, sir." I waved a hand in the direction of the closest bar. "Lead the way."

He patted both my and Marlo's backs before walking briskly between us, the two of us following behind like a couple of well-trained dogs. To be honest, I had absolutely zero desire to do shots tonight, but once again, I found myself unable to say no to his request. If the big boss wanted to toss back copious amounts of straight liquor with his employees, then down them we would. It wasn't like we really had a choice in the matter.

As we headed toward an overly crowded bar up ahead, my thoughts drifted back to Lily. I hoped like hell I wasn't missing my chance with her and that she'd still be there when this was all said and done, like I'd asked. I also prayed

I wouldn't be a drunken fool by the time I got back to her. The last thing I wanted to do was get too inebriated to tell her how I felt. A little liquid courage was one thing, but being plastered beyond the ability to function properly was a line I had no intention of crossing. I had to get out of this in one piece.

"I think the boss is trying to get us drunk," Marlo shouted toward me with a shit-eating grin on his stupid face.

He unbuttoned the top two buttons of his dress shirt, and I watched as a plethora of chest hair sprang out, no longer kept hostage by the thin material.

"Sure looks that way," I said with an annoyed groan.

"What's your problem, Maguire? Lily's not going anywhere. And if she does, you know where she'll be come Monday morning."

That was the second time he'd brought her up in less than a minute. I tried to shrug it off, but Marlo irritated me more than anyone else in the office. Some guys you got along with, and some you just plain didn't. Marlo and I fell into the latter category, and my dislike for him had been fueled once I learned he wouldn't help Lily transfer out of P&D. Ever since then, I hadn't been very good at faking niceties with him when all I wanted to do was punch him in the mouth.

"You don't know what you're talking about, so how about you just shut up?" I ground out through clenched teeth as we came to a stop in front of a busty blonde bartender wearing a flapper dress that wasn't loose like they typically were, but clingy and barely covered her ass. As a matter of fact, it didn't cover it at all whenever she bent over.

Even at one of our *classy* affairs you couldn't escape the typical LA woman looking for her big break, sporting a fake tan, fake nails, fake hair, and fake tits.

No, thank you.

"Stop being a prick." Marlo punched me in the shoulder, and I bristled.

I will not lose my temper. I will not lose my temper, I chanted to myself silently, for fear that if I stopped saying it, I just might.

"Cheers." Our boss shoved what looked like bourbon or whiskey into our hands.

"Cheers," I said in return before sending the amber liquid down the back of my throat too quickly.

Bourbon.

Nothing burned the way bourbon did if you didn't take your time with it. It wasn't meant to be a shot that you tossed like it was your last chance at breathing. And those who did shoot it were idiots. Bourbon was meant to be savored, breathed in slowly through the nose, and then sipped at like a fucking gentleman who appreciated the value of time and a good drink.

"One more!" my boss shouted before ordering another round from the blonde, who was currently staring at me and batting eyelashes that couldn't be real.

I tried to look as uninterested as possible, hoping she'd take a hint, but women like her tended to be a little relentless, used to getting what they wanted when they looked like that. Yes, she was pretty. But in a completely typical and store-bought way.

We drank another shot, again tossing it back the way it was not meant to be drank, and I needed to hydrate if this wasn't going to end anytime soon. One more shot turned into three, and by the time I was allowed to leave the bar and get back to my Lily, I had no idea how much time had passed. My gut warned me that it had been too much, that I'd taken way too fucking long.

I sprinted up the winding staircase, stopping once or twice to make sure I didn't fall. The stairs were blurry. My balance was wobbly at best.

Damn bourbon.

When I reached the open space at the top, my hopeful heart sputtered and then died. She was nowhere to be found.

"Lily?" I said into the void, glancing around the shadowy corners just in case she was hiding somewhere I couldn't see, like she had done when I first left her.

But she wasn't.

Running around the small area like a madman, I said her name, pulled back curtains, and peeked behind fake doors, but she wasn't there.

She wasn't anywhere.

She hadn't waited like I'd asked her to. Then again, she wasn't a pet I could command to stay put until I returned whenever it suited me.

But damn, I desperately wanted to finish what I'd started with her earlier. *What if that was my only window of opportunity? Why did my boss insist on drinking so much bourbon? Why haven't I learned my lesson* yet? My head spun with the barrage of thoughts and the realization that I could probably use something to eat to help soak up all the alcohol currently swimming in my near-empty stomach.

Moving toward the ornate railing, I looked at the crowd below, my eyes searching for any sign of Lily's red dress or her long, dark hair. There were too many people. Too many red dresses. None of them attached to her.

Marlo suddenly appeared at my side, a plate filled with appetizers in one hand and a drink in the other. "Here.

Figured you could use something to eat."

He shoved the plate at me, and I took it without question even though I had no idea why he was up here or why he was being somewhat pleasant. Maybe he was even drunker than I was. That was the only plausible explanation.

"Thanks," I said as I stuffed the bread and seafood pastries into my mouth. "I needed that."

"I figured. The old man likes to get us fucked up. I think he gets off on showing us how much better he can handle his liquor than we can," he said, his words not slurring, but coming out far slower than usual. Like it had taken him a lot of effort to say them in the right order.

"I'm just glad he let us walk away while we were still standing this time." I finished off the last item on my plate, feeling much better already. It was amazing what a few carbs could do.

"So, what are you doing up here all alone? There's, like, a hundred beautiful women downstairs you could be sweeping off their feet," Marlo asked, and I instantly became suspicious.

I didn't want a hundred other women; I only wanted one. And he knew it. He was baiting me to say it.

Fuck it.

"I was looking for Lily," I finally admitted out loud.

He didn't look even remotely shocked. "Where'd she go?"

Shaking my head, I stared at him. "I have no idea."

"She was up here with you earlier. I saw you guys kissing maybe?" he said, but it was definitely a question and not an assumption, which surprised me.

Marlo was always such a colossal asswipe, saying whatever asinine thought came into his head with no regard for the damage it might cause. I refused to let Lily be one of his verbal casualties.

"Yeah, she was up here. No, we weren't kissing," I clarified.

"Well, where'd she go, man?" he pushed.

I turned, a little defensive. We weren't friends, but he was acting like a concerned one, and that confused me.

"I said I didn't know."

"You're not even trying to find her." He shoved me out of the way, his drink almost spilling as he looked past the railing where I had just stood, doing the same thing.

"Why do you suddenly care so much?" I asked, trying to figure him out.

Marlo wasn't usually the guy I trusted with anything, let alone my personal life.

He turned to face me. "Because I know you're into her.

And I'm so sick and tired of watching you do nothing about it. The two of you just go round and round," he started to explain before looking back down into the crowd. "Shit, dude."

I ran to his side and stared down. "What? What is it?"

"She's with Colton fucking Adams." He jabbed a finger into the air and pointed into a sea of people off in the distance somewhere.

How had he spotted her so easily when I couldn't even find her, no matter how hard I searched?

And just like that, my eyes landed on her and …

You've gotta be fucking kidding me.

COLTON FUCKING ADAMS

⭐ DECLAN

LILY WASN'T JUST with Colton Adams; she was attached to his right arm—literally. He had her wrapped up at his side, like she belonged there.

How the hell did that happen so fast? Or maybe it hadn't been fast at all. *Had I really been gone long enough that it gave Colton a chance to swoop in and steal my girl?*

Hell, a single minute was probably too long to leave a woman like Lily alone. Especially the way she looked to-night. If I hadn't known who she was, I would have wanted to. And I bet that was exactly what Colton had thought when he looked at her. Like she was a prize to be won, a winning ticket to be claimed, a gorgeous woman he just *had* to meet.

Colton Adams was one of the hottest actors of our gen-eration. Tonight's party was themed around the box-office smash that he had starred in and won an Oscar for. And he was currently focusing all of his attention on my girl, his head turned toward hers as he listened to her with raptly and clung on to whatever she was saying. And from my vantage point, she was clearly enjoying it. Not that I blamed her entirely. Colton had a reputation for actually being a decent guy, and the few times I'd been able to meet him in person, he actually had been.

Just my fucking luck, right? The least he could do was be a complete douche bag and give the rest of us poor schmucks a chance.

As Lily stood next to him, her head tilted back in a laugh, Colton's free hand moved to rest on her lower back, like my woman was his to touch and hold. Jealousy and competition seared red hot through my body like a flame, burning everything in its wake to ash. The way he held her was definitely more than a little friendly, giving off vibes to anyone who looked at them that they were an item—or at least coupled up for the night.

Fuck. I'd lost my dream girl before I got the chance to have her.

I slammed my fist on the handrail, thankful that our set builders were top-notch. Another set might have crumbled under my hit or at least started cracking but not ours.

"Why are you still standing here? Go get her. You know

you want to," Marlo egged me on.

I turned to face him with a scowl. The last thing I wanted was him in my personal business or giving me any sort of love advice, but he seemed hell-bent on pushing me in Lily's direction tonight, and I had no idea why.

"What's your play here?" I all but growled at him.

His face pulled together in confusion. "My play?"

"Yeah. What's in it for you if Lily and I get together? It's not like you can take my job—we're equals. So, how do you benefit?" I asked, sounding like a dick. I'd never completely trusted Marlo before, and I wasn't about to start now.

"Dude"—he almost looked offended—"there's no play. Promise." He held up the hand holding his drink in some sort of salute. "Plus, why would I want to lose Lily? She's a great assistant. Everyone loves her."

"Tell me about it." I nodded back down to where she stood, still next to Colton and his throng of fans.

He laughed before smacking me a little too hard on the shoulder. "Listen, the entire office knows you're in love with her. We're all tired of waiting for you to make a move already."

My jaw dropped open slightly before I clamped it shut and argued, "You don't know what you're talking about."

"Oh, please, Declan. You think we don't see you go all googly-eyed for her the second she steps into a room? It's almost embarrassing."

My fists clenched at my sides as I contemplated hitting him, simply to get him to shut up, but not because he was wrong. I thought I'd hidden it well, but apparently, I didn't hide shit when it came to her.

"You're an idiot."

"No, you're the idiot if you don't go get her. She likes you too. You're just too dumb or stupid to see it."

I squared my shoulders to face him, our heights almost perfectly matched.

"Or maybe you're just too scared."

"Scared of what?" I spat.

He shrugged. "I don't know. But come on, Declan. Let's go. I'll be your wingman."

Why was he giving me a pep talk like some sort of emotional sensei? While I wanted to believe that his intentions were good, I honestly couldn't decide whose side he was on.

"Colton Adams can get any chick he wants. He doesn't need yours. Don't let him take her."

"Leave me alone." I tried to wave him away, but he refused to leave.

"Pity party for one, your table's ready," he yelled through a guttural laugh.

"Shut up."

He ran his fingers through his jet-black hair and breathed out heavily in my direction. "Stop being a pussy and go get her before he takes her home and fucks you right out of her thoughts. I never took you as the kind of guy who gave up so easily."

The thought of Colton fucking Lily yanked me out of the state I had been in. That woke me right the fuck up. "I'm not."

"The hell you're not. You're standing here, feeling sorry for yourself, when you should be down there, taking what's yours," he practically spat.

"She's not mine," I said, hoping to remind him that Lily didn't belong to me, no matter what lies I told myself.

"And she never will be if you let that shit continue." He waved his hand in the direction of where Lily and Colton stood, still looking far too comfortable with one another. "Go and seal the deal already."

Everything Marlo had said either encouraged me or pissed me off. There was no in-between.

"I'm not trying to seal any deal, so stop referring to Lily like some cheap piece of ass I'm trying to bed and then forget."

He choked out another laugh, his shoulders bouncing up and down, like I was the most hilarious person in the room. Then, he finished off his drink and dropped it on a table. "Just do us all a favor, please, and at least make a move. This cat-and-mouse game between the two of you has gone on long enough. You're killing us."

And then it hit me. Those fuckers had bet on us. It wouldn't be a far-fetched notion, considering that we tended to bet on all sorts of stupid shit in the office behind closed doors. Like how long it would take our old vice president to start nailing his brand-new assistant. Cliché as hell, but I'd only lost that bet by two days. But I had won the one on how long it would take for his wife to find out and file for divorce instead of forgiving him and letting him come back home.

Of course, this had all been before the two interoffice dating experiences gone wrong. I'd thought we stopped placing bets on those kinds of things after that happened.

"Do you have money riding on this or something?" I asked, and he took a step back, his expression like a kid who'd gotten caught stealing candy.

"Not anymore. You took too long."

"You assholes bet on us?"

"More than once," he said with a cocky grin, and I

flexed my hands before balling them tight. He glanced down, noting my fists before he continued, "Don't be pissed, man. We all just saw it coming and had a little fun, like we usually do."

I stepped toward him, puffing out my chest like some sort of caged animal. "Don't ever bet on my personal life or Lily's again, you hear me?"

"I hear you," he said before reaching for his empty glass and pouring the droplets of melted ice at the bottom into his open mouth before putting it back down.

"But you don't care?"

"Not if you don't go get her, I don't," he said with a smug smile. "Don't be that guy."

"What guy?"

"The guy who gives up without a fight," he said matter-of-factly before focusing his attention back down on Lily and Colton, knowing damn well that I'd do exactly the same.

I wasn't an insecure guy by any means, but when I compared myself to Colton, the way I was currently, I suddenly felt like I didn't add up. Why the hell would Lily St. Claire choose me over a guy like that? Who in their right mind would pick a regular, everyday guy over a rich and famous actor who could give her the world?

I growled to myself, debating on how to handle this situation. Watching Lily down there with him was killing me. If there had been rocks on the ground, I would have started kicking them like a petulant schoolboy, hoping to get her attention in the process.

My heart pounded in my ears, the sound drowning out almost everything else in the room. I hated to admit that Marlo was onto something, but he was. When had I ever backed down from a fight? Was it because my competition was some metrosexual pretty-boy actor with more money than God?

Shaking my head to right my senses, I swallowed deep and sucked in a swift breath, one mission in mind. "Fuck it," I said, and Marlo slapped his hands together, knowing he'd won. "Let's go."

TYPICAL AND CHEESY

⭐ LILY

I HONESTLY HAD planned on waiting right where Declan had asked me to until he came back and finished what we'd started. There was nothing I wanted more. But then Colton Adams was crooking a finger at me and calling me downstairs for some reason. And in some strange twist of fate, I'd found myself doing exactly that … leaving the balcony and moving through the crowd toward the direction I hoped Colton was in.

I felt a sharp tug on my arm, stopping me short in between a group of large men I didn't know and couldn't place. I gasped in shock at first, violently shaking my arm to release it from the hold before looking up to see who was manhandling me. Colton Adams's crystal-blue eyes were staring at me, his mouth twisted up in an amused smile.

"Did I hurt you?" he asked as he leaned toward me, his

voice thick and rich and utterly recognizable from all the blockbuster movies he'd been in. If I closed my eyes, I'd still know exactly who was speaking.

"No, you just startled me, was all," I said, feeling a little bit starstruck.

Colton Adams was downright gorgeous and not stick thin or short, like most of the other celebrities I'd seen on the lot.

"I shouldn't have just grabbed you like that, but you were walking so fast, and I didn't want you to get away after I asked you to come down here," he explained like it all made perfect sense when it made none.

I stared at him, listening to the way he spoke. It was an odd thing—to be around someone you'd only seen in movies in real life. They talked and moved the same way they did in their box-office hits. I forgot for a second that I was having a conversation with Colton Adams and not a character he played.

"Do we know each other or something?"

Maybe he had me confused with someone else. It happened to me a lot. Apparently, I had one of those faces that people always said looked like someone they knew. There was no other logical explanation for what was currently happening or why he'd summoned me to his side.

He smiled again, his eyes looking me up and down. "We don't know each other, but I wanted to change that." He extended his perfectly manicured hand in my direction. "I'm Colton," he said as though I was possibly the only person on earth who didn't know his name.

I smiled in return, my hand reaching out for his. *Soft.* His hands were so soft. Probably softer than mine, and that was all kinds of wrong. He might not be the version of pretty like the other actors were but supple hands meant that he most likely didn't like to get dirty.

I bet Declan gets all kinds of dirty, I thought to myself before remembering that Colton was waiting for me to tell him my name.

"Lily," I said, noting the fact that not a single spark had ignited with our touch.

I'd assumed that coming into contact with this gorgeous specimen of a man, I'd at least feel something resembling lust. But no chills raced through me, no bolts of lightning zipped, and no erratic heartbeats. The only thing I had felt was general attraction, but anyone with the gift of sight would be attracted to this man. He was simply that good-looking. Almost too good-looking, if you asked me. He was like a freaking work of art, and I found myself staring, wondering how it was possible that someone could be made this perfectly.

"A beautiful name for a beautiful woman," Colton said before kissing the top of my hand, exactly where Declan had kissed it earlier. The exact same spot!

Sadness ripped through me when I realized that Declan's lips weren't the last to touch this particular piece of my skin. Skin I hadn't planned on washing and now wanted to wash clean. Shaking my head to rid myself of such juvenile thoughts, I grinned at Colton and thanked him for the compliment as I pulled my hand away and rubbed it with my thumb. Angry. I was angry that he'd stolen Declan's kiss from my hand. Angry that he'd taken something that didn't belong to him. I was being silly, and I knew it, but I still couldn't help it.

"So, what do you do, Lily?" Colton asked, his chiseled body still angled toward my own as he reached for my arm and placed it in his.

I briefly considered pulling it away but didn't want to cause a scene, so I kept it there as I leaned toward him, so we could actually hear each other over the noise of the party.

"I work for the studio," I shouted as pride filled me.

Even though I didn't love my actual job position, I adored working for this company. I knew how lucky I was to be part of such a coveted studio. It seemed like everyone in the entertainment industry wanted to work here at some point in their career, and I was one of the ones who actually got to.

"Do you enjoy it?"

"I love it," I said before glancing around, looking for any signs of Declan but failing to see him. There was no way I'd be able to find him in this madness. Not only wasn't I tall enough to see over people's heads, but there were also waytoo many here to find one in particular. I resigned myself to the notion that I'd most likely never see Declan again until we were back at the office on Monday morning. I wondered what that would mean for us.

Would he still want to finish what he started, or would we pretend it never happened?

"I bet it's a great place to work," Colton added, bringing my thoughts from Declan back to the heartthrob standing near me, who should be eliciting far more of my attention.

"It is. What about you? Do you love being an actor?" I asked before feeling rather stupid. Who the hell wouldn't enjoy acting? But I didn't know what to say to someone like him. It wasn't like we had anything in common.

"I do actually." He lowered his lips toward my ear, and I found myself leaning away slightly with his nearness. "I get to meet beautiful women like you every day and come to really great parties like this one," he said with a wide smile, and instead of finding his response charming, I found it somewhat off-putting.

Thats what he loves about his job?

"You really are stunning," he said once more, and I let out an uncomfortable breath.

If I had been a little enamored by Colton Adams when he first called me down here, it was quickly losing its luster. Cheesy pickup lines didn't do anything for me. Neither did compliments about my looks, which I had little to no control over. That type of flattery meant nothing. This guy didn't know me. Saying that I was beautiful was superficial, sur-face level, *easy*. Call me crazy, but I'd rather be complimented on my brains or my witty personality.

My grandmother always reminded me that looks faded with time, but who you were on the inside never truly went away. It was one of those things I always held on to … and valued when it came to men.

Glancing around the party once more, I realized again how futile of an effort it was to look for Declan, but I couldn't seem to stop myself. I wanted to find him. It was him I wanted to be standing next to, not this movie star who meant nothing to me.

"Am I boring you?" Colton asked, and I laughed.

His question hadn't even been that funny, but for whatever reason, I couldn't stop myself from tossing my head back and laughing like it was the funniest thing I'd heard all night. Colton's arm wrapped around my back, and instead of moving out of his grasp, I stayed put, my arm gripping on to his shoulder for balance.

"You're not boring me. I was just …" I thought about lying to him but realized that I owed this guy nothing, no matter who he was. "I was looking for someone."

"And that someone isn't me?" He batted his eyelashes, and I rolled my eyes to stop myself from groaning.

"I didn't even know you before ten minutes ago," I said, and he nodded.

"But you know me now. We could get to know each other better." He raised his eyebrows, indicating that he was serious and asking me. When I didn't immediately respond, he phrased the question differently. "Lily, do you want to get out of here?"

GET MY GIRL

✦ DECLAN

MY FEET HIT the bottom floor, and I was instantly turned around in the moving crowd, having no idea which fucking way was the correct one. It was a clusterfuck down here, and I'd lost Lily as soon as I couldn't see her anymore. Glancing behind me, I was thankful for once in my life that Marlo was following close, moving me by the shoulders in what I hoped was the right direction. I pushed and shoved my way not so gentlemanly through the throngs of bodies, apologizing as I walked even though I wasn't even remotely sorry.

I spotted Colton and Lily up ahead, his hand still splayed across her lower back. Still unsure as how to handle the situation, I decided just to go for it. I was thankful that Lily's arm was no longer on his shoulder or slung through his other arm. Her hands were now clasped together in front of her body, holding a small black purse for dear life.

Is my woman uncomfortable?

I stopped for a second, and Marlo leaned toward me. "Go. I'll be here if things get hairy. I've got your back."

I nodded because I was too caught up in the moment to disagree with him or say something snarky in response. My legs moved of their own accord.

"Hey, Colton." I stepped between him and Lily, separating their bodies with my own before giving him a smile and a nod that warned him not to fuck with me.

His face pinched together with my movement, his body language turning defensive, like I'd offended him somehow when it was clearly the other way around.

"Do I know you?" he asked.

"No, but you have something I want." I glanced at Lily and watched as her face paled slightly, her eyes widening with shock.

"Oh yeah? What's that?" Colton cocked his head to the side before I extended my hand toward Lily and held my breath, waiting for her to either say something or take my hand in response.

Colton turned his attention toward her, still in a defensive position, as if he were protecting her from me. "You know this guy?"

Her hand reached for mine, her fingers intertwining between my own as I pulled her swiftly away from Colton's frame and into mine.

"I do," she said, her eyes locking on to mine with surprise and heat.

She loved what I'd just done. It was written all over her face.

"Is this who you were looking for earlier?" he asked her, and she bit her bottom lip and nodded. "You're a lucky guy," Colton said with an incredulous smile that basically said, *Congratulations, you win!*

"You're telling me. Excuse us. We need to go," I said before leaving him there to find someone new to flirt with.

He was done taking what I wanted.

As I attempted to navigate through the crowd yet again, this time with Lily at my side, she tugged on my hand to get my attention.

"I can't believe you just did that." Her voice hit my ears, and I stopped walking immediately and grabbed her face with both hands.

The crowd had to move around us, two bodies standing perfectly still in a sea of people meeting and greeting and dashing off to who knew where.

"I couldn't stand there and watch you with him any

longer. I was losing my damn mind."

I refused to wait. Not for privacy, not for anything. I'd been waiting for two long years. I took her mouth with my own, kissing her senseless and reveling in the fact that her eyes had closed before I even touched her. I closed mine, too, completely lost in the moment, as her mouth opened to welcome me, her tongue pressing against mine. The things I wanted to do to that tongue.

Fuck.

The things I wanted to do to her body.

She was pressed against me, her hips already grinding into mine, and I was harder than I could ever remember being. I knew it wasn't the time or place to be putting on a show, but in the moment, all logic and reason were tossed out the proverbial window. I finally had the girl of my dreams in my arms and to hell with who saw us.

ONE HELL OF A KISS

✦ LILY

*O*H MY GOD. I was standing in the middle of the biggest party, Declan's tongue in my mouth, and I couldn't get enough of it. I never wanted it to stop. I gave thanks to the wish I'd made earlier on that fake falling star, convinced that it was responsible for what was currently happening. Pressing my body against his, I could feel every hard inch of him, and it only made me want him more. His dick was thick and pushing against the fabric of my dress, and I couldn't seem to stop my hips from grinding in little circles.

His fingers fisted in my hair as he arched my neck back, placing kisses there and biting as I moaned before reality crashed down around me. Opening my eyes, I noticed that people were staring, so I pulled away from him, forcing our fused bodies to disconnect.

"Declan," I said, but it came out in barely a whisper.

"Not here, I know." He squeezed his eyes closed before reopening them.

Reaching for my hand once again, he maneuvered us through the crowd. I glanced up at the staircase and noticed my boss standing there, watching us a little too closely. He gave me a thumbs-up, and I didn't know what to do in response, so I looked away quickly.

"Marlo just gave me a thumbs-up," I yelled at Declan.

"Yeah. I'll tell you about that later," he shouted back at me, still leading us in some direction I couldn't even see.

I had no idea where we were headed, but as soon as we walked outside and the night air hit me, I shivered. "Where are we going? I'm going to freeze to death out here, Declan."

He wrapped his arms around me, his body pressing against mine as his heat spread across me, his dick still hard. I loved knowing that I had done that to him.

"I need to get you alone. I was going to take you back to the office. Do you think that's weird? It's probably weird, huh? It was just the only place where I figured we'd have some privacy. Quickly."

His office.

Our department.

Where I'd daydreamed about fucking him twenty ways

to Sunday.

"That's fine," I said, stopping myself from salivating.

"Good," he said before slipping out of his suit jacket and placing it across my shoulders. I wrapped it tight around me, buttoning two of the top buttons before Declan threw his arm around me and tucked me up against him. "I swear to God, no one had better be in there."

I laughed before growing a little nervous.

What if this is all built up in my head? What if this doesn't mean anything to him and is just a one-night stand? What if I'm just something he needs to get out of his system with no intentions for anything more?

Oh my God, I had so many questions and no answers, and I was going to lose my mind by the time we actually reached his office.

I stayed quiet, keeping the million questions in my head at bay while he basically dragged me as fast as I could walk in high heels toward our building in the distance.

"Almost there," he said, and I hummed out my response, acknowledging that I knew.

"Want me to carry you? Am I walking too fast?" he asked, and I giggled before stopping.

"No, but let me get these off. It will help." I lifted one foot up and unfastened the buckle before doing the same with the other. Holding the pair in my hand by the straps, I felt free.

"Those shoes are sexy as hell, Lily." Declan licked his lips, and I had to stop myself from hopping into his arms and wrapping my legs around him like a belt.

Those exact words could have come out of Colton's mouth, and I would have been slightly offended, but hearing them from Declan turned me on. It was funny how the same words might feel different depending on who was saying them.

We walked through the open breezeway of our building and into the elevator as the emotions swelled between us.

"I want to kiss you so bad, but," Declan started to say, and I knew what was coming, "cameras."

"I know."

There were cameras in every elevator and security guards who kept an eye on the footage twenty-four hours a day, seven days a week. There was no reprieve or keeping anything a secret once those doors closed.

The elevator dinged, and we stepped out into a completely dark room before the motion-detecting lights flickered to life, announcing our arrival. Declan pulled open the door to the wing of our department, and I walked through it, thankful to see that it was pitch-black. That meant that no one else was here. The lights continued to come to life as we walked hand in hand down the long hallway, neither one of us saying a word. The mood was intense, my emotions escalating with every step.

When we reached the door of his office, Declan pulled out a set of keys and unlocked it before holding it open for me with one hand. The door closed behind us, and he locked it.

"Just in case," he said, and I was grateful for the extra caution as I dropped my heels onto the floor.

There were no windows in Declan's office that faced inward. In other words, no one could see us from the interior of the building, but he had one hell of a view, facing out. The hills were dotted with the houses, and fireworks sporadically went off in the distance. I'd almost forgotten that it was New Year's Eve when my mind clicked into place.

"What time is it?" I asked, and Declan had already taken off his jacket and was sitting on the two-person couch in the center of his room.

"It's only ten thirty," he answered with a sweet smile that made me want to kiss him again. "We still have time."

"Time for what?" I asked, not really sure what he was referring to.

"The countdown," he said, and I felt myself get all giddy

inside. It was ridiculous, but it couldn't be stopped. "You want to kiss me at midnight, don't you, Lily?" he asked, his voice husky and turning me on even more.

"I've wanted to kiss you at midnight for the last two years," I said without thinking.

It was the truth, but I hadn't meant to admit it so easily, without being pressed or at least hearing him say it first. With no response, Declan extended his hand and waited for me to take it. I hesitated for only a moment before giving in. The second we touched, he pulled me straight onto his lap, but I was unable to move the way I wanted to in my dress. I felt his hardness and stopped myself from groaning out loud or reaching out and grabbing it.

"Lily," he said my name like it was his bliss, his hand resting possessively on my back to stop me from going anywhere.

When did he start saying my name like that?

"Declan." I could barely respond, the size of his member making all rational thoughts fly out of my head and filling it with dirty ones.

"I have to be honest with you … I'm having a really hard time controlling myself right now." He picked me up like I weighed less than nothing and moved me to the side of him, our legs still touching even though I couldn't appreciate that fact through the fabric of both of our clothes.

I watched as he ran his fingers through the strands of his dirty-blond hair, and I found myself wanting to do the same as the weight of his words hit me.

"Why are you trying to control yourself? I thought the whole reason you brought me back here was to lose control." I knew I was teasing him, tormenting him even, and I liked the way it made me feel a little powerful. Like I was somehow in control of this entire situation when I knew it wasn't true and that I'd give in to whatever he asked of me.

He blew out a quick breath as he stared through me, his gaze piercing something deep inside of me and stirring it to life. "I did. But damn, Lily, I can't believe this is actually happening."

There it was. The admittance that revealed my own inner dialogue.

"You can't believe it? How do you think I feel?" I asked through my surprise.

"I'm just lucky you haven't left yet," he said, sounding completely serious, and I couldn't stop the small chuckle that escaped from my lips.

"Why would I leave? I've wanted this for years."

"Me too," he said, and my breath got stuck in my throat as I gasped. "Don't you know how I feel about you?"

"How *you* feel about *me*?" I asked incredulously. "How would I know something like that?"

He reached for my neck and held me with one hand, like he couldn't believe I was real. "How can you not? Apparently, everyone knows. I'm the office joke because I can't hide my feelings for you." He tried not to sound offended, but it looked like he was embarrassed.

"Well, you've done a good job, hiding them from me. I had no idea. I thought you didn't really even see me." I shook my head because it hadn't come out right. "As more than an assistant, I mean," I attempted to explain.

He made an awkward and uncomfortable sound. "Didn't see you? Hell, Lily, all I fucking see is you."

I felt my cheeks heat as my eyes started to water. This was all so much at once, but I'd wanted it for so long that I didn't want him to stop talking.

"You don't hate me, right?"

"Hate you?" I looked deep into his bright green eyes and made sure he heard what I was about to say. "I've never hated you. Why would you ask that?"

He pulled his hand from my neck and cocked his head to the side, as if he was measuring his words before he said them. "You always looked at me like …" He paused. "Like you wished I would be dismissed or go away and leave you alone."

"What?" I practically spat because I had no idea that I'd ever looked at him in any way other than with downright lust. "Dismissed? I don't even know what that would look like," I stuttered. "But maybe it was in response to the way I thought you looked at me," I confessed, a little embarrassed.

"And how did I look at you?" he asked, his eyes piercing mine, and I had to look away from them to break the trance and answer.

"Lately, it's like you're disappointed in me," I said. "Almost like I make you sad or something."

"Disappointed?" He reached for my chin, tilting it up so he could touch my lips and press a soft kiss there. "Never."

"Then, why the look?"

He sucked in a breath, his hand still holding my face. "I think it's because I knew you wanted to move into another department and your dumbass boss wouldn't let you. Each time I saw you, it reminded me that you wanted to be doing more and you weren't being allowed to. It pissed me off. I had to walk away from you every time the thought entered my head."

His words struck an all too familiar chord inside my heart. I'd felt the exact same way over the past year but never had the guts to confront Marlo about it—or anyone else for that matter.

"I had no idea you knew about that."

"Ellen let it slip one day."

"Ah, Ellen." I nodded in understanding. "So, you're not disappointed in me then?"

"Only if you won't be mine," he said before closing the space between us completely and taking my mouth again with his.

Talk time was officially over.

Thank God.

My lips parted without question, giving him the answer he'd already known. His hands wrapped around my waist as he pulled me back onto his lap, my dress still way too tight to straddle him the way I craved. Pulling the fabric up, I placed my hips right where they needed to be as my legs clasped around his lower back. My dress could rip into a thousand pieces at this point, and I wouldn't care. Declan's breath was hot, his tongue wet as he kissed my neck and bit my ear before claiming my mouth once more. I was eager and all too willing, my body writhing against his, letting him know how badly I wanted him inside me.

Stopping the whole thing entered my mind for point-two seconds before I pushed that ridiculous thought out of the way and told it to go to hell. This wasn't just some random fling or one-night stand with a guy I'd just met. No, this was Declan Maguire. The man I'd wanted for so long, who wanted me the same way back.

He was my New Year's wish come true.

FINALLY

✦ DECLAN

THIS—RIGHT HERE, RIGHT now—was what I'd fucking dreamed about for the last two years. Lily St. Claire was wrapped around me, and I never wanted her to let go. She felt so damn good, her hips grinding softly against me, my hands squeezing her ass so hard that I might leave fingerprints.

"Are you okay?" I asked, making sure that we were on the same page. One that included me being inside her the moment she let me.

"More than okay," she said, her voice breathy and worked up. I fucking loved it.

I nipped at her neck, the salt of her skin fueling me further. "I've wanted you since the day I first saw you."

"What took you so long?" She pulled away with a grin, her brown eyes filled with something more than lust.

There was no good answer to that question.

"I'm an idiot. Clearly. But I'm here to make up for lost time, if you'll let me."

"Oh, I'll more than let you," she whispered as she brought her face back to mine.

Her lips crushed against my own, her tongue running across my bottom lip before moving inside my mouth like she knew every inch of me already. Damn, everything this woman did turned me on. Every. Single. Thing. She was my kryptonite, and I'd gladly go down in flames because of her.

Having Lily's body grinding against me caused a silent war to start waging within me. My dick wanted me to strip Lily naked and fuck her silly on the floor of my office *right. This. Second.* My head warned me that it probably wasn't the best idea. Not to mention the fact that our first time shouldn't be on a fucking office floor. The third or fourth time, maybe, but not the first. She deserved something far more romantic than being bent over my office desk for our first time. Although damn, that would be hot.

My dick complained and fought valiantly, growing harder as I elicited sounds from Lily's throat that made it difficult to maintain reason, but I persevered, dammit, because I was in charge, not my dick.

That was a lie.

"Lily." I pulled her head away from mine. It was painful, having her move away from me instead of moving closer.

"What's wrong?" she asked, her brown eyes lit up with concern, like I'd changed my mind or something as equally as awful.

"Nothing, love." I kissed her cheek. "We don't have to do this here." I cupped her face, my thumb tracing her jawline.

"Yes, we do."

"I only meant that if you didn't want to have sex for the first time in my office, I'd understand," I added, trying to be a fucking gentleman but she was making it hard.

"I want to," she said, and I laughed out loud.

"You do?"

"Do you have any idea how many times I've fantasized about you fucking me on that desk?" she asked as she pointed to it, and that was all I needed to hear.

Permission. Granted.

Grabbing her in my arms, I pushed to a stand and stalked over to my desk, tossing the papers and shit on the floor before laying her body on top of it.

"This isn't going to work," I complained, and she sat up.

"What do you mean?"

"That dress," I growled. "I need it off."

"Oh." She got a little sly look on her face before she gave me her back. "Unzip me, please. Or tear it off. I don't care."

I reached for the zipper and lowered it, kissing her back with each inch of perfect skin revealed to me. *Fucking goddess.*

"All done," I said as I pulled at the fabric, wanting to see it on the floor instead of still on her body.

Lily stood up, and it fell, just like I'd hoped. Red pooled on the ground as she stepped out of it, nothing but a matching red strapless bra and lace thong covering her.

"Jesus." I'd meant to say it in my head, but it came out of my mouth.

"Like what you see?" She hopped up on the desk and sat up straight, her legs crossing.

"Love what I see." I emphasized before grabbing her legs and forcing them apart, a giggle escaping her perfect fucking lips.

I stood between her open thighs and lowered my mouth to her tits, kissing at them through the fabric of her bra before taking it off with one hand. They sprang free, all full and luscious and begging to be played with. I kneaded her left tit as I took her right one in my mouth and started sucking. Her nipple was hard as I rolled it around with my tongue and bit it lightly. Lily moaned, her head tossing back as pleasure tore through her. I switched from the right to the left, giving it equal attention and love. The sounds she made just from me sucking her tits almost made me come in my pants, but I wasn't done with her yet.

Dropping to my knees, I heard her suck in a gasp, her hands instantly fisting in my hair. I reached for her lace thong and pulled as she writhed underneath me, helping. Pulling the fabric down the length of her legs, I planted wet kisses and licked my way toward her feet before removing them completely and tossing them off to the side somewhere.

I'd dreamed of this moment—tasting her, eating her, fucking her senseless. Taking one glance up at her, that look in her eyes, her lips parted, I couldn't wait a single second longer. I dived toward her pussy and took my first lick. She practically screamed out the second my tongue touched her.

"Gotta stay still, love," I warned, and she tried to stop her hips from gyrating as I plunged my tongue inside her.

She tasted like fucking heaven. *Delicious. Perfect. Mine.* I licked her up and down, my tongue only stopping to fuck her with it in hard and sharp movements before I added a finger. That set her off. If Lily had been forcing herself to have control, she'd lost it the moment my finger entered the mix.

I fucked her with my finger, making that crook to hit just the right spot as I licked her like I might die without her taste on my tongue.

"Oh fuck, Declan. Yes. Jesus. Just like that." She pulled my hair, and I thought she might rip some of it out.

I didn't give a shit. She could have it all if she kept saying my name like that.

"Oh God. I'm gonna come, Dec. I'm gonna come," she said, and I fucked her faster with my finger, ate her harder, and sucked on her clit.

She came apart in my mouth, writhing, moaning, panting. Her hand slammed down on my desk, the loudness a shock to my system as I stood up slowly and wiped at my mouth with the back of my hand.

"Damn, Declan," she said between labored breaths. "That was so good. You're so good at that."

I'd take the fucking compliment every day of the year from her.

"There's more where that came from," I promised because I'd live the rest of my life eating that pussy.

"Me first." She grabbed my pants and started to work at the button before I stopped her.

"I can't," I said.

Her eyes pulled together. "You can't?"

"I'll come in five seconds if you suck my dick, love. I need to be inside you."

"Oh. Well, in that case." She dropped her hands completely and leaned back on the desk and waited while I slowly got undressed, not allowing her to touch me until I was completely naked.

When I pulled down my pants and removed my boxer briefs, I watched as her eyes widened—she clearly approved of what she was seeing.

Thank God. It wasn't like I could change the size of my cock.

"I don't have a condom," I said, hoping that she was on the pill or something.

"I'm covered. And I'm clean."

Music to my ears.

"Same."

I leaned over her body, and when I went to kiss her, she didn't pull away. It turned me on even more to know that she could taste herself on my tongue and she wasn't repulsed by that fact. She kissed me even harder as I reached for my cock and guided it toward her entrance.

The head of my dick barely touched her, and she was

already trying to scoot closer to get me all the way inside.

"I want you, Dec," she moaned.

I pressed myself against her and tried to go slow, but she was so fucking wet that I couldn't wait. My cock went all the way in until I couldn't go any deeper, hitting her wall. Her pussy clenched around me like a glove, all tight and warm, and I thought I might have said her name, but I wasn't sure.

"You feel incredible," I said as I moved in and out of her, the pressure already building. It had been too long since I'd had sex. My hand definitely didn't count, and I was paying for it now.

"You feel amazing," she said in response, her hips moving in time with mine.

We continued this way, me pounding into her on top of my desk, the drawers slamming open and closed. It was the only sound aside from the ones coming out of our mouths.

"Fuck, Lily. I'm not going to be able to hold out much longer."

"It's okay. Come in me, Dec. Fucking come in me," she ordered, and I absolutely fucking lost it.

My thighs burned as I continued thrusting, my dick getting even harder before it exploded like a volcano inside of her. On shaky legs, I finished before the rest of my senses started coming back to life. My heart was racing, my dick was pulsing, and my head was spinning.

"You are the most incredible woman," I said between breaths, and she laughed.

"I literally did nothing but sit here," she tried to say, her own breathing strained.

"Your pussy was made for me."

"I think your dick was made for me."

"Then, it's a good thing we found each other, huh?" I teased before standing upright and staring down at my still-hard dick, soaking wet with desire and juices.

"I should go to the bathroom and get cleaned up," Lily said as she stood and stretched her arms out over her head in all her naked glory.

"Go before I ravish you again," I teased, and she looked nervous.

"What if someone comes up? I should get dressed?" she said, but it came out like a question.

I agreed. There was no way in hell I'd let someone from the office see my girl naked. I was losing my mind, just imagining it.

She quickly pulled her dress on, sans bra and panties, and scooted out of my office. Sex filled the air, and I wondered if it would be gone by Monday or if I'd still be able to smell her the second I stepped through the door.

BETTER THAN DREAMS

⭐ LILY

WALKED OUT of Declan's office and toward the bathroom in a daze. I'd actually done that—had sex with my crush, on his desk, like I'd fantasized about a hundred times before. It wasn't a dream. Hell, it was better than any dream my mind could have conjured up. It was mind-freaking-blowing—thank God. Hands down, it was the best sex I'd ever had in my life.

Not to mention, the oral. That man knew how to eat a woman out. My knees grew weak, and my sex tingled, just thinking about it. The light refused to turn on when I pushed open the bathroom door, so I reached for the button and pressed it, hoping I wasn't going to have to go pee in the dark. It flicked to life, and I hurried into the stall before washing my hands and wetting a paper towel to clean myself up a bit.

I had no idea what we were supposed to do now, but there was no way I was letting Declan leave here without me. We would be starting this new year with a bang. When that clock ticked down and moved us forward another year, I wanted to be in Declan's arms. Or in his bed.

Smiling to myself, I exited the bathroom and headed back to Declan's office, where I saw him sitting on the couch, looking downright ravishing. His pants were pulled on but unbuttoned. Same for his shirt—on but open to reveal his muscular pecs and stomach.

He was a vision I wanted to feast on until I died from it.

"Did you want to go back to the party?" he asked, his eyes searching mine for what seemed like some kind of clarity. Maybe he was second-guessing what we'd just done.

"Not really. Do you?" I asked as nerves infiltrated my senses.

"No." He smirked.

"Do you have any suggestions then?" I asked as I moved toward him and sat.

He ran his fingers through my long hair, and I was thankful they didn't get caught up in my hair-sprayed strands.

"We could go back to your place?" I suggested tentatively. *What if he wants the night to end here? I will die from freaking embarrassment.* "Or mine?"

When he didn't respond right away, I started thinking about somewhere neutral instead. "We could go get something to eat maybe?"

He laughed out loud, like I'd just offered up the most hilarious of things to do. "I was just trying to remember if my condo was a mess or not." He kissed my mouth once more, his lips lingering as his tongue moved back inside, deepening our connection.

"Declan," I said as I pulled away, not wanting to read into anything. I needed to know where we stood.

"Are you having second thoughts?" he asked as he cupped my face.

Me?! I wanted to scream.

"No. Not at all. I was actually wondering if you were."

"Not in a million years," he breathed out before kissing me again, the passion unmistakable and undeniable.

He was as into this as I was.

"Good," I said with a smile. "And I know that we aren't supposed to date internally. Do you think we'll get in trouble?" I asked even though I was more concerned about him losing his job than me losing mine. Not that I thought he was more important than I was. I guessed it was just second nature for a woman to want to nurture and put others above herself.

"It's a good thing you'll be transferring to another division then, isn't it?" he said.

I reared my head back in shock. "What? Who said I was transferring?"

He leaned back into the couch, his hands never breaking contact with some part of me. "I did. Worked it out with Marlo tonight. He agreed to a recommendation for you as soon as you want one."

My eyes started to water. No one had ever gone to bat for me before. "Seriously? You talked to him for me?"

"I'd do anything for you. Don't you get that by now?"

His words made me feel like we'd been a couple for decades as opposed to having just slept together for the first time mere minutes ago. There was something so refreshing about feeling that comforted, that secure.

"I can't believe you did that. Thank you." I pressed a kiss to his cheek, his stubble rough against my lips. "Do you think we should put a pin in this"—I waved my finger between us—"until I transfer out? I'd never forgive myself if something happened to your job."

"Not a chance," he said without even taking a breath.

"You're sure?" I questioned again, refusing to be the one who put his position in jeopardy even though I wanted him to not care about it. When it came to us versus work, I wanted us to win.

"It will be fine. People have dated internally before. It ended badly because they were dumb. Plus, you can't stop two people from falling in love with each other," he said easily and without pausing, and my eyes grew wide as his words slammed into my heart like a sledgehammer to the chest. "I mean … you know what I mean." He tried to cover but stumbled.

I swallowed hard, torn between telling him I loved him back and keeping my damn mouth shut. "Right. Of course. So, they can't fire us for dating?"

"Hell, Lily, I guess, technically, they probably could. But I won't let it happen, okay? The big man likes me." He pressed another kiss to my lips. "I'm not letting you get away from me now that I have you. And I'm not waiting until you transfer departments. I've been patient long enough." His words were delivered with force, as if me believing them meant everything to him.

I stayed quiet, soaking in the moment, the afterglow, the strength of his convictions, but he must have misread my silence.

"Do you want to be with me?" he asked.

"Oh my God, yes," I said with a small sigh at the end.

"It will be okay. We'll be okay. We won't get in trouble."

"You're sure?"

He straightened up for a second and inhaled long and deep. "Do you want me to get permission first? I mean, tell me what you want me to do, and I'll do it. If you want me to ask Richard, I'll ask him. I don't care, Lily. You're worth it."

"I'm sorry, Declan. I'm not trying to be annoying. I just don't want us being together to be a bad thing," I admitted, and his hands were in my hair again, running through the strands like they were the most fascinating thing in his immediate grasp.

"Us being together could never be a bad thing. Please stop worrying. I won't let anything happen to either one of our jobs, okay? I promise you that."

I opened my mouth to argue, or complain, or say the opposite just to say it when he pressed a finger against my lips to stop me from talking.

"I said, I promise. Now, do you want to get out of here or not?" he asked with a wink.

"Hell yes," I agreed a little too excitedly before adding, "I wished for this, you know?"

"For what exactly?" he asked as he started to button up

his shirt.

"For you."

"When?" He stared at me, waiting for my response, as if he already knew.

"Tonight. They had shooting stars, and I wished for you. I mean, I know they weren't real," I started to explain, but he cut me off with a laugh. "Don't laugh at me, Declan. I'm trying to be sweet here."

"I'm not laughing at you," he said before pressing a kiss to the tip of my nose. "I wished for you too. On the same fake stars."

"You did?" Chills raced through me.

"I did. Come home with me, Lily."

I answered with a nod before leaning up on my tiptoes, the muscles in my neck straining as my lips crushed against his and my hands wrapped around his neck to pull him down to me. We stayed like that, lost in the moment, in that kiss, our tongues dancing, before I broke it.

"What time is it?"

He reached for his phone and cocked a brow. "Eleven thirty."

"How long will it take to get to your place?"

"Ten minutes," he said, and I believed him even though nowhere in LA took ten freaking minutes.

"If you don't kiss me at midnight, we're going to have a big problem."

"I'm going to kiss you every midnight on New Year's Eve from tonight until I die," he said, and my heart grew ten times bigger with his words.

I'd always sensed that this was more than a crush, something more than lust, but after tonight, it was confirmed. Declan was meant to be mine. And as we walked out of his office hand in hand, I knew I'd never be able to look at this hallway or department the same way again … especially the desk in his office.

EPILOGUE

LILY

ECLAN HAD MADE love to me three more times that night. I'd never experienced anything that intense before. Sure, I'd had good sex, but this was different.

Everything about Declan was different. He was strong but shared his feelings with me. I never questioned where I stood with him or how much I meant to him. Declan not only told me, but also showed me with his actions.

He was an absolute catch, and I was never letting him go.

Everyone in the P&D department had known the minute Declan and I had gotten together even though I'd thought we'd been careful about our relationship and tried to keep it on the down low. No one cared, and we never got into any kind of trouble over it—thank God. I had been sincerely worried that at least one of us would take the brunt of breaking an unspoken rule. But now that I was in another division of the company, I didn't have to worry anymore.

I'd ended up transferring to the theme parks division six weeks later with my boss, Marlo's, blessing, recommendation, and help. I knew Declan had talked to him about it, but he insisted that Marlo was the one who had stepped up and actually made the switch happen. I wasn't sure I believed him, but my man usually didn't lie. I guessed it didn't matter how it had all gone down; all that mattered was that it finally had. I was currently a marketing assistant on the fast track to becoming a manager and eventually a supervisor.

I was happier than I'd been in a very long time, working where I felt like my talents were actually being put to good use and so in love that I could barely see straight. Dreaming about being with Declan had been one thing, but real-life Declan had proven to be so much more fulfilling.

We were a good team, supportive of one another and both equally driven in our own ways. Whenever we weren't at the office, we were together, usually at his place. He'd even given me my own key and told me to move in whenever I was ready. I'd been ready the first night he brought me home, but I tried to maintain some sense of calm instead of telling him I'd go grab my things and be right back.

Falling into a rhythm with him had been almost

effortless. I supposed that was what happened when you found your perfect match, the one you'd wished for on fake falling stars.

I wouldn't have it any other way.

THE END

Thank You

Thank you so much for reading this story. I hope you enjoyed meeting Declan and Lily as much as I enjoyed writing them. I came up with the idea for my Fun for the Holiday's Collection to give you lighthearted, happy reads that you could get lost in. I know that the world has been crazy lately, hopefully this helped you escape… if only for a little while. <3

About the Author

Jenn Sterling is a Southern California native who loves writing stories from the heart. Every story she tells has pieces of her truth in it as well as her life experience. She has her bachelor's degree in radio/TV/film and has worked in the entertainment industry the majority of her life.

Jenn loves hearing from her readers and can be found online at:

Blog & Website:
www.j-sterling.com

Twitter:
www.twitter.com/AuthorJSterling

Facebook:
www.facebook.com/AuthorJSterling

Instagram:
@AuthorJSterling

25822698R00078